Hysteria 4

Winning short stories, flash fiction and poems from the

Hysteria 2015 Writing Competition

The Hysterectomy Association and sponsored by Covance UK Ltd.

Edited by Linda Parkinson-Hardman

Hysteria 4

Published by: The Hysterectomy Association

ISBN: 978-0-9927429-7-3

A catalogue record for this book is available from The British Library.

Telephone: 0843 289 2142

Website: www.hysterectomy-association.org.uk

All characters in this publication are fictitious and any resemblance to real persons, living or dead is purely coincidental.

Cover Image: © Boule13 | Dreamstime.com

About the Hysteria Writing Competition

Hysteria is an annual writing competition for women only; it opens on the 1st April each year and closes at midnight on the 31st August. You can find out more about the competition, including rules and guidelines for entries on the Hysterectomy Association website about the next competition at: www.hysterectomy-association.org.uk/hysteria-writing-competition.

Acknowledgements

The competition and this anthology wouldn't have been possible without the support and help of all the following people.

This book is dedicated to them and to the users of the Hysterectomy Association.

Thank you. Linda Parkinson-Hardman (editor).

Judges

Short Stories:

Tracey Glasspool	Clare Girvan
Ginna Wilkerson	Tamara Jones
Ayalla Buchanan	Lucy Williams
Sal Page	

Flash Fiction:

Helen Chambers	Emma Norry
Diane Simmons	Lyndsay Wheble
Ninette Hartley	Sarah Eaton
Elizabeth Ducie	Lizzie Heasman

Sade Norwood

Poetry:

Janet Dean	Mandy Huggins
Vicki Morley	Marion Spencer
Eithne Cullen	Sarada Gray
Samantha Read	Clare Archibald

Foreword

It has been a privilege for me to be among the first to read the stories and poems compiled in this book. The wit, creativity and inventiveness of the entries has made all of us at Covance very proud to sponsor the 4th Hysteria Writing Competition.

Across each category, be it flash fiction, poetry or short story, a theme that has leapt off the page to me is that of strength, particularly strength in the face of the adversities which we as women will face throughout life. Though they may not always shout about it, or even fully believe it, the women in this anthology (and their fellow men!) show an indomitable spirit. And I think that's something we can all relate to!

The judges have done an excellent, if unenviable job of selecting this year's winners, and have also included some sage advice about writing across all of the categories. For anyone considering submitting an entry for the 2016 Competition, their words are a good place to start.

The pieces in this compilation have played on my mind, resonating with me for several days after reading, and whetting my appetite for what the competition has in store for the years to come. And I hope it will have the same effect on you, too.

Ruth Smethurst
Covance Clinical Research, Competition Sponsor

Contents

Flash fiction

The Flash Fiction category was open to entries with a maximum word count of 250 words. These ultra-short stories needed to be complete and give the reader the satisfaction of not being left hanging.

The challenge when writing flash fiction is to tell a complete story in which every word is essential. It's important that the writer pares down the padding, peels away the layers and ends up with the pure essence of the story.

Advice from our Flash Fiction judges

Ninette Hartley

www.olivespastavino.com

Judging the Hysteria Flash Fiction Competition was an interesting experience and I enjoyed it immensely. It was surprising how many entries had the same or similar theme and very few of them made me laugh or smile, I would have liked a few more of those please, it doesn't all have to be doom and gloom to be a good read. The ones that stood out for me were written clearly with no ambiguity involved, those that made me think and stayed with me and the few that made me smile. One piece of advice, if you are going to write something with a twist, however slight, get someone to read it without the ending and see if they can guess what it might be, then you'll know whether or not your twist is going to work. Make sure your theme is clearly portrayed, being confused by a short story is not at all satisfying for the reader. Read your story aloud to other people and it will soon be obvious if you've got it right or not.

Elizabeth Ducie

www.elizabethducie.co.uk

I read a lot of short stories as a competition judge, not just for the Hysteria Association, but for other organisations as well; and I find two common issues with many of them.

Firstly, they are depressing. So many focus on death, disease, dementia, child abuse etc—or even a combination of these themes. Of course, these are very real issues and can lead to powerful writing, but they don't make for easy reading—especially when a judge has a couple of hundred or more to go through. And I should add that while this is a personal opinion, other judges I have spoken to feel the same way.

And secondly, they are predictable. There is a common belief among writers that there are only seven stories in existence—and I see no reason to argue with this belief—but there are an infinite number of ways in which these stories can be retold. Far too often, I read the opening of a story and predict what it's going to be about and what the ending will be.

Now, I'm not suggesting that a downbeat story with a familiar theme is not going to be a winner. In some cases, the writing is so good it just can't be denied. But I am suggesting that an upbeat story, especially if it makes me laugh out loud, is much more enjoyable to read; and if the theme is less obvious, and the ending is unpredictable, so much the better.

So next time you are planning to enter a competition, why not spare a thought for the judges' happiness—and surprise us by making us laugh and surprising us with an unusually twist to your tale.

Lyndsay Wheble

www.lyndsaywheble.com/

It was a pleasure judging the Hysterectomy Association Competition's flash fiction strand in 2015, but several things came up again and again that I'd advise any entrant to avoid:

Twist endings. Personally, I find little more frustrating than having a piece hook me in with a theme, a character or atmosphere, just for it to be dashed in the final few sentences. To me, it comes across as cynical and uncommitted. A good piece of fiction should be a revelation, not a trick.

Vaguely-drawn sentimentality. Many of the pieces concentrated on familial or romantic relationships, which are great topics to explore, but there was a tendency towards exaggerating the emotions or situations into the realm of the mawkish, whilst not putting enough work into the illustration of why the relationships in question were so special to the protagonist. Relationships need to be enacted in fiction to be believed, and offsetting any overt sentimentality in your work with a dose of reality or contradiction will usually serve to elevate it, making it much more effective.

Common topics or themes. It is not difficult to anticipate when entering a writing competition who the market for it might be, and therefore, what subjects they might write about. In this competition, there was an overwhelming number of pieces about women getting their groove back, leaving husbands or losing husbands, or discarding familial obligations in favour of new lives. Some of these pieces were great pieces of writing, but the similarities between them worked to the detriment of all, as they all started to blend together. Try and anticipate this and write something that will stand out.

Emma Norry

www.linkedin.com/pub/emma-norry/81/851/230

This is an exciting category to judge but reading the variety of entries, it did strike me that there appears to be some confusion amongst writers regarding exactly what flash fiction should be!

Flash fiction does not *have* to have a twist, and in fact, it's difficult to do this effectively in a unique way that doesn't feel a 'cheat' to the reader (this was all a dream/narrating from beyond the grave/think narrator is a child but it turns out to be a pet/adult etc... we came across these examples multiple times!).

Flash fiction is not a 'slice of life' (this is a vignette). Flash fiction should still be a complete story with a beginning, middle and an end. Due to the brevity of flash, the form is not an effective form for multiple characters, multiple locations and/or heavy dumps of backstory.

Flash fiction can be the perfect format to also 'play with' language in a way that one might not have the opportunity to do so in a longer form – in other words, you can explore familiar topics but in an unusual way. The entries from the writers who chose to explore language in this way leapt out immediately.

Helen Chambers

www.about.me/helen_chambers

Every word has to count, so use them sparingly and carefully. Revise and edit! I'm put off immediately by grammatical errors, so proof-read properly. An unusual or off-beat story which stayed in my mind for hours, or even days, after the first reading, always scored more highly.

Sarah Eaton

www.saraheatonwriter.wordpress.com/

I really enjoyed judging, but there were highs and lows. Sometimes I read something and got goose bumps because it was so good, a complete whole. Other times though a piece of flash fiction would build up and up, then leave you hanging with neither conclusion nor intrigue, or go off at a complete tangent. Remember that there is no room for any filler in a piece of flash fiction. That sounds so obvious but it is worth repeating.

In terms of advice, what this all means is read, read, and read it again. Put your story in a drawer so you unearth it anew, post a copy to yourself, email it to yourself. And don't be afraid to change things. Keep a couple of different versions saved on your laptop. Last and most importantly be yourself.

Diane Simmons

dianesimmons.wix.com/dianesimmons

I think that it's often what you leave out in flash fiction that's important. With so few words you have to let the reader do much of the work, but it's important that the story is actually a story and goes somewhere. There should be some development, no matter how small. Realistic dialogue (if used) is vital for me to enjoy a story and characters should be well developed. The best stories I read for the competition managed to do all these things, as well as produce a good ending. But many of the stories failed to finish well - often I was hooked by a strong beginning, only for it to lose momentum. It's vital too that the ending is not just a trick or something that comes out of nowhere.

He Loves Me, Not

Gayle Letherby

www.twitter.com/gletherby

I toss the decimated daisy on the pile of others.

A list might help.

PETE

Tall, toned. Long hair. Sparkling blue eyes. A generous smile.

Clever. A PhD student. Plays guitar, enjoys sport, loves Babe his sports car.

Tuesdays, Thursdays, some Sundays. Countryside drives, gigs at the SU, walks in the park. We laugh a lot. He strokes my face, kisses me softly, asks about my dreams and describes his research ambitions. No talk about us.

JASON

Tallish, nice bum. Thinning hair. Brown eyes. A chin dimple.

Clever. Something in the bank. Enjoys reading, loves films, supports Man City.

Wednesdays, some Fridays, an occasional Sunday. Cinema and pub trips, walks in the park. Kissing until my lips are swollen. He talks a lot about his work and about our future together.

A decision.

Dear Pete

I like you a lot. You're lovely. We have fun. But I want to settle down. I've met someone else who might like to settle down with me. Don't think badly of me. Be happy. Beth x

Pressing SEND I hear the ping alerting me to an incoming email; two in fact.

Dearest Beth

I'm too nervous to say this so I'm trying email. I LOVE YOU. Let's make plans, live with me, marry me. Let's have babies, trade in Babe for a Four-by-four.

Say yes, make my day, my life. Pete xxxxxxx

Beth, I can't see you tomorrow. I'm married. She knows. Don't contact me. No hard feelings. J.

Karma

Eve Brimacombe

It used to make me queasy when he ate with his mouth open: glimpses of churning food, saliva bubbling round his teeth, the odd semi-masticated, sodden crumb that would cling to his lips or the corners of his mouth. The accompanying sound track was nearly worse, a sickening symphony of slurps and chomps followed by lip-smacking and satisfied burps and belches.

Then one day he caught my look of revulsion. The crack of his hand across my nose knocked me off my chair and in a second he towered over me, panting heavily, his breath rank as he spat those same crumbs into my face and cursed me; cursed my careful upbringing that had given me 'posh lady muck' ideas about eating and manners and behaviour. He cursed and ranted, his stubby fingers laced through my hair, pulling my scalp taut as he pounded my forehead repeatedly against the leg of the table, until the blood ran down my face and my right eye swelled and closed. From then on I kept my eyes averted and my expression neutral during meals.

My sister called it karma when he fell from the scaffolding. He still eats with his mouth open, and I watch as indifferent carers ladle mushy pap between his sagging lips, and briskly wipe away any excess spittle and drool. His eyes bore into me, black, vengeful and brim-full of helpless, impotent fury, but now I only smile. These days I no longer mind the sight at all...

Out of Sight

Susan Howe

At last the crying has stopped and all she can hear is the percussion of shingle in surf. With each ebb of the tide her troubles drift further away, carried on a dazzling web of light. Knee-deep, she sways, mesmerised.

A whistle rouses her. She watches a terrier bound into the waves and recalls Joe's remark after another sleepless night, "Should have got a dog instead".

She squints towards the town, where her husband has gone for ice cream. When he gets back I'll tell him I've changed my mind, she thinks. She imagines his delight. More than anything she wants to hear him laugh again.

In the distance a familiar shape shimmers like a mirage emerging from the heat and her heart leaps the way it used to. She pictures her husband's face and body; tastes the salt on his skin.

Waving, she runs to meet him, eager to share her decision. She fancies he'll choose a big dog; a labrador, perhaps.

She sees his eyes widen, then narrow, as she approaches.

"It's all right, Joe," she calls. "Everything's going to be all right."

Her husband stops, stares, drops the ice creams, and rushes forwards. She follows his gaze to their belongings, out across the bay and back, giggling as he grabs her shoulders and shakes her, a little too hard.

"Jess. Where's the baby?"

Her smile doesn't falter as she reaches for his hands. "She's gone, Joe," she says. "I changed my mind."

My Angel

Clare Graham

www.twitter.com/writing_clare

Apple and cinnamon; I know it's her before I turn. Dappled light falls on folds of a cream dress, freckling its pale green border. A single rose in her hand, my angel stands bathed in pied light. Without my camera, I must capture her in my head.

Our relationship ended years ago, but we've met every summer. It's impossible not to love her still.

"Another year gone," she says. "Jamie, you're the only constant thing, and that's special. Knowing you'll be here, no matter what." Her touch; always gentle, always warm, soothes as nothing else can. But sunlight is dancing across a diamond that's taken the seat of our tiny gold band.

"He's not you, I know that. My heart was broken. It took me ages to see. And he's kind. Don't think of him as taking your place, but as something uncultivated; and for me, well, pioneering: a little happiness maybe, before I'm through." Her words race, blurring the image in my head. I should respond; wise words, an encouraging embrace. My voice remains hidden under a veil of time and space. As pixels decompose, haze creates distance, like travelling through a tunnel. A dark shadow is clouding the edge of my vision.

Wait! What can I do? Don't shut me out. I love you. The words I want fall softly on moss and grass.

"Don't believe I'll forget. It's just...time," she says, placing the rose at the foot of my grave before linking arms with the shadow.

The Reunion

Damhnait Monaghan

www.twitter.com/downith

Stella is nearest the door; my old pal from the bank. She was with me that first jittery day, her mere presence boosting my confidence. Now she looks tired and worn out.

On the other side of the room I spot Chloe, still sexy after all these years. Late nights and strong cocktails never bothered Chloe. I used to lie in bed Sunday mornings, jaded and spent. Chloe was more resilient: a quick wash and she bounced back. We went to some incredible parties together, including the one where I met James.

And there, draped on a chair in the corner is sassy Victoria. There was a time when she knew all my deepest secrets. She was along for the ride the first time I went to James's flat, the first time we … my cheeks burn at the memory.

I hadn't expected to see these old friends when I came up to the attic; it really is time to say good-bye. My Stella McCartney suit doesn't work for the school run or cheering Jack from the touchline. The Chloe dress still fits, but I stopped wearing it when Polly said black made her tummy sad. I grab a box to pack up my cast offs, resolving to bring them to the charity shop in the high street. Well, maybe not all of them; I'm keeping the Victoria's Secret number. I think it's time she and James got to know each other again.

Sunday Racers

Alex Reece Abbott

www.alexreeceabbott.info

The old lycra-skinned men swoop down the vale, sweeping her off Route 65.

Bold in their anonymous pack, helmeted and be-goggled, they override her right-of-way. A wannabe-Wiggins breaks ranks, pausing to bellow abuse at her for failing to respond to their near silent approach.

Grunting, legs pumping, the rest of the fluorescent herd whooshes past her, marking the cool Sunday morning air with sour sweat, hyper-floral laundry powder and sickly Lynx.

Banished to the brambled, muddy margins of the path where once the Scotsman flew, she watches the brash competitive Cyclops racing to join his peers. An angry red eye flashes from his rear, fading until finally it vanishes on the horizon. Sans teeth, sans bells – sans a six year-old's manners - the bilious eighteen-wheeled beast terrorises any pedestrians, driving them from his path.

She kicks the mud from the soles of her boots. Perhaps they never had bikes when they were boys, she thinks, Perhaps they never knew the kiddish joy - the liberation of going on a long-as-it-takes-adventure, making it up as they went along, seeing who could pedal to the top of the steepest hill and then savouring the simple reward – the fresh breeze caressing their faces as they free-wheeled down the other side.

I forgive you, she thinks. She adjusts her hearing aid and walks on into the head-wind, pondering what a walking stick might achieve when applied to a fast-moving set of carbon fibre spokes by a stupid woman with a well-hidden taste for retaliation.

When Trisha Became Pat

Alison Wassell

alisoninwriterland.blogspot.co.uk

'I can call you Pat or Patricia,' said Miss Pennington, on the first day of term. Trisha, who had always been comfortable with her name, became Pat.

Pat became the kind of girl who featured in books by Enid Blyton. She was a 'brick' and a 'good sport'. She was the captain of the netball team, and shouted 'Good try!' when other girls failed.

Pat draped her cardigan around her shoulders, in imitation of her teacher. She 'popped to the loo' rather than 'going to't bog'. Pat's family laughed, at first. Later they became angry.

'I've half a mind to go down that school and tell that teacher what I think of her,' said Pat's mother. Pat smiled, knowing that she never would, being possessed of less than half a mind, and lacking the words to compete with Miss Pennington.

'Always aspire,' was Miss Pennington's motto. She too had come from a 'low class background'.

Miss Pennington was not done with her own aspiring. She left at the end of term, for a school in a leafy suburb.

Pat baked cakes, as a parting gift. Miss Pennington dabbed away a tear. She would keep in touch, she promised, although she offered no address. Pat left the classroom with a smile, sensing that a hug would be inappropriate. Through the glass panel in the door she watched Miss

Pennington pick up the cakes and drop them into the bin, smacking her hands together. Pat was always known as Trisha, after that.

The Invisible

Sally Jubb

www.sallyjubb.com

The girls kneel in long rows.

'Let us pray.'

Parquet bores deeper into sinew, cartilage and bone. Angela wonders (apart from the heap of black rags slumped in a chair) why the nuns are allowed to stand.

Hail Mary...

She watches Margaret Jackson's legs, remembers them in emerald, doubleted and hosed; detects a fleshy tremble through the prefect's tunic, imagines creamy thighs, a trellis of downy hair. A dimple.

Full of grace...

As some pray for gymkhana victory, others for perfect breasts, Angela, ignominious by dandruff and spots, plays Portia to Margaret's Bassanio.

Blessed art thou among women...

Margaret prays for her father.

Blessed is the fruit of thy womb ...

That before nightfall he will be crushed under the wheels of a train.

'All rise.'

With bland smiles, 3B file file beneath the gaze of Sister Dympna, who, from the stage, scans sock lengths, skirt-hems, souls. Some, with lowered lids, affect meekness. In vain.

A cry! Sister Dympna's milky finger is pointing at Angela Dyer's feet. The finger curls in, pulling back towards the milky face.

Angela treads the wooden steps silently, majestically.

Pray for us now...

Sister Dympna's hand presses hard across her lipless mouth, her eye fixed upon Angela's shoes: stack-heeled, two-toned, with brazen stitching (they almost resemble leather).

... and at the hour of our death.

Angela bathes in the quivering silence, unholy, effulgent, until Sister Dympna's eye, unseeing, swivels right, to a thing that is growing beneath Margaret Jackson's tunic. Angela is invisible once more.

King of the Castle

Vanessa Savage

www.twitter.com/VvSavage

My cardboard castle has turrets and a flag on top. It's the best castle in the world – Mum got me the boxes and helped with the cutting out but I put it together myself on the front lawn.

"That's a nice palace."

I look at the man who spoke. His hair's tangled and he looks dirty. Mum says don't talk to strangers, but she also says it's rude not to speak when spoken to.

"It's a castle, not a palace," I say.

"Sorry… I live in a box too, but mine's not a castle." Close up, he doesn't smell that bad – no worse than Billy in school. He's biting his lip, just like I do.

Mum comes over. "Hi Pete." If she knows his name, he's not a stranger.

"Why does he have to live in a box?" I ask after he's gone.

"He didn't always," Mum says. "He had a castle of his own once, but the silly man gambled it all away."

Next day, I drag my castle out onto the pavement and wait for him to walk by again.

"You can have it," I say. "A castle all of your own."

Mum's always telling me our house is our castle. One castle is enough for me and it's nice to share.

Mum's calling me so I skip back up the path, leaving the man holding his castle. It looks like he's crying and I bet it's because he's happy. I hope he doesn't lose this one too.

Factory Gate

Jacqueline Cooper

www.catelyncash.co.uk

I am in the supermarket when the factory siren sounds. Conversations stop dead as all heads turn towards the window and huge building on the hill that dominates our town.

Mine isn't the only hand reaching urgently for my phone.

No message. The siren stops abruptly but echoes on in my pounding heartbeat.

In the school, well drilled teachers will be soothing anxious pupils, while surreptitiously checking their own phones.

In the hospital, emergency staff will be gearing up.

I abandon my purchases and walk out of the shop. I'm not alone. Others, white faced, climb into their cars. Vehicles pull over to allow us to leave. The drivers have seen our expressions. They know where we are headed.

I think of breakfast this morning, turning away from his kiss. The angry slam of a door and I whisper a prayer.

Reaching the factory gate, I join the gathering crowds. Lots of familiar faces but not the one I'm looking for.

I push forward till a policeman stops me.

'My husband-' I can barely choke the words out.

'What's his name, love?'

I tell him.

He consults a list. Something flickers in his eyes. He shows me to an office but his professionalism slips when I hear him murmur. 'Keep her here till someone comes to talk to the widows.'

The widows?

I stagger, burying my face in my hands. Hiding the bruise on my cheek. And my relief.

Poetry

The poetry category sought entries which had a maximum of 20 lines, not including spaces. Many of our entries followed a strict rule of either four or five line stanzas, but a few challenged this convention.

Poetry is not something that can easily be defined; but it is a written form which lends itself to being spoken out loud. Sometimes, it is easier to understand poetry when you hear it, rather than read it because the rhythm and emphasis of the words can be more easily defined.

The poet's challenge is to create a strong visual image and emotional reaction in the reader or listener.

Advice from our Poetry judges

Janet Dean

thepracticeofwaiting.wordpress.com/

I enjoyed reading all the poems, but when I found those that really connected, the experience was beyond enjoyment, it was joyful. It's not so much about shared experience, as about recognisable emotion, and you can feel this coming through when a poet really lets go. When writing, I often start with an idea and then just free write for as long as I need to without stopping or lifting my pen from the paper (or my fingers off the keyboard). I then select and sculpt the poem from this raw material, sometimes pushing and urging it to come, but other times just finding it there, and letting it happen. Be natural, be honest, be yourself.

Eithne Cullen

Throughout the process I felt privileged to be reading poems of such high quality, many expressing and exploring deep issues. I was impressed with the way poets dealt with themes of love and loss, illness and death. At this stage, it might be right to advise "avoid cliché" in your poems, but I was impressed by the lack of cliché in many of the poems I read, and the fresh way emotions were explored. There were some very novel themes explored; as someone who sometimes wondered "Why are there no poems about periods?" I was happily surprised to see the subject up for discussion as well as a poem which reminds us of the discomfort of waiting for a scan with a full bladder. Many poems were in strong, first person voices, and women's voices were strong in their representation and messages.

There was a small number of poems where some obscure reference or strange context made reading challenging but, in these, the rich language and careful form often compensated for the work involved. Some readers might not work so hard, so it is worth checking that the content is not in-accessible, when the writing has taken such effort and skill.

Mandy Huggins

troutiemcfishtales.blogspot.co.uk

I was honoured to be asked to judge this year's Hysteria Poetry Competition.

At the start it felt like a daunting challenge: would I find poetry with that indefinable magic, with original language, arresting imagery and adventurous ideas to surprise me? Would I be able to identify the poem that - for me - shone above the rest?

For a poem to work the poet needs to communicate with the reader, not just talk to themselves. Beautiful language is meaningless if there are no concrete ideas and no clear message. The best poetry is never overcrowded, the words are reduced to an essential essence that dances to a unique rhythm.

There needs to be a confident voice, and even if that voice is a delicate one, it needs to have surety.

But a winning poem needs more than deft technique, originality and a clear message. It has to resonate, demand re-reading, it has to touch the soul and linger in the mind.

The main themes amongst this year's entries included the usual suspects: death, marriage, funerals, war, friendships and adultery. There were also poems about rats, FGM, social media, and even a hallway chair. Universal themes will always outnumber the quirky and unusual, but they need to be approached with fresh eyes to be noticed.

There were several great poems in the competition, but a couple shone above the rest for me. The first concerned a modern day Bonnie and Clyde - a fresh and poignant twist on the theme of wild youth being shot down by real life in all its mundanity - the bullets of mortgage, marriage, kids and career. The other was inspired by a recent news story - an evocative story of loss and longing, of enduring love and the sea. At the heart of both of these poems is hope...and a sprinkling of the Poet Fairy's special dust.

Vicki Morley

I have a brief couple of sentences to help writers, as I think most know the obvious ones, like follow the rules...

Writing a poem for a competition is an opportunity to review what you have written that might fit the theme, if there is one, and then the chance to revise, check and check again. A poem that you feel is your best is the one to enter.

Darwin said that we only notice the unusual. As a judge I was looking for a poem that showed new light on an old subject or was totally unique. The best advice is read more poetry, keep writing and enjoy it.

The Weight of Glass

Sue Spiers

www.twitter.com/spiropoetry

A glacial cylinder with its thumb-thick base,
its circumference weighted to balance a hand's span,
mazarine reflections of the fjord's ice.
The fire-pit spits out sparks of moonlight.
My tongue courts the contents of the glass;
A dalliance of lakkalikööri, a sting, a glow.
glabrous swirling coats its inner skin;
reminders of cold nights encased in your arms.

Calling off the Wedding

Debs Riccio

debsjriccio.wordpress.com

She can imagine her mother
twisting her rings, patting her curls,
playing with her glasses,
brushing her lap free of lint
as she makes this weekly phone call.

She can imagine her mother's
heart plummeting, hopes crashing,
dashing down to her soft-slippered feet,
as thoughts of her new outfit, freshly-pressed
and hanging on the wardrobe door,
fly past her face like a great floral bat.

She imagines the roaring noise
her mother's disappointment will make
as it spools up the miles between them
before settling like a damp dog,
dejected at her feet.

Walking

Cath Blackfeather

cathblackfeather.blogspot.co.uk

The woman walks, she walks
A hip-swaying
Loose-spine
Summer-day walk.

She don't come-hither,
Don't- you- want- me walk
Nor oh-I'm -so-scared-
They- might-look- at- me walk.

She swaggers.
The woman swaggers.
She don't
Blokey-stiff-knees-all-shoulders-my-balls-are too-big
Swagger.

She swash-buckles
Horn-swoggles
I-own-my-street,
spine-unravel, breathe
And fill-my-space swaggers.

Older

Wendy Locke

Dancing through decades in my pixie boots,

breaking down my Berlin walls, bearing the world
on padded shoulders, Rubik's dilemmas
solved, or so I thought. In truth sliding
into deep abyss, scrabbling for the edge,
fingers raw, or teetering on a tightrope
made of string. Those decades danced before me.
Now, I'm mother, laughter etched in melting face.
The cord has long since shriveled, my children,
with children of their own, harboured under
bat wing arms, my joints make themselves known.
Yet, I am only halfway to my grave,
my heart is not yet grey, feet fervent to foxtrot,
I dance on, content in cushioned soles.

By The River

Maureen Gallagher

amazon.co.uk/maureen-gallagher/e/b002j6d06y/

A group of young women with kids,
camped by the riverbank, watch
the drift of cloud, the water lick
their toes, when a sudden sound
back beyond the long grass,
warns of how a current can take
a child off to a bed of sedge,
weed and algae – down to the dark.

A mother skims the stony ground,
broken, brittle, likely as glass
to rip a bare sole. She swoops,
to find her son alone, not lost,
just playing out of view. She rests;
examines her feet but not a mark.

My little sister is 44.

Janet Lee

janetlees.weebly.com

The thought flew out
of the bathroom mirror
like a trapped bird
released.

We used to run across flat rocks
on our Spiderman feet
to where the sun-dried surface slicked into black
and limpets clung in blind huddles

just ahead of the incoming tide.
Creeping up, we'd knock them loose with stones
and offer live sacrifice to the gulls;
our hearts loud and hard as their dinosaur calls.

The thought shifts, washes
through me, fills my mouth and eyes.
My sister, 44, not running anymore;
clinging on just ahead of the incoming tide.

Are you safe? I want to go home.

Abigail Wyatt

(for Yuko Takamatsus who was lost and Yasuo Takamatsu who searches
for her)

The sea is beautiful. She is beautiful.
It seems he cannot say 'was'.
He is stuck in that moment when her living fingers,
each with its pale, tender moon,
would not be silenced but spelled out nimbly
despite the biting cold, her last, bright star
of hope and sent it like a prayer into the void.
She was high up then, halfway to heaven,
her dark head crowned by clouds;
how the wind must have roared as the ocean
ate away at the ground beneath her feet.
Now he trawls for her memory,
pitches himself backwards,
heels over head towards the sea-bed.
"I have this feeling.' he says.
'It seems to me that still
she wants to come home.'

Read the news story here: www.bbc.co.uk/news/magazine-33294275

Winter's Gift

Nicola Warwick

www.twitter.com/warwick_nicola

You pronounce it the perfect kind of snow, scoop
some in your hands, squeeze it tight
until it compacts to an opaque knob of ice.

I can only think of your gloves, soaked by meltwater,
the cold of your palms, how your fingers will ache
when you dry them back to life.

But you're more man than that. You embark
on a silent sculpting of ice, that little lump
becoming something more than white matter from the sky.

Your hands move with the speed of a magician.
The sun is thawing the snow; we are surrounded
by the drip drip of water in a brief taste of warmth

before the day fades. You give me the slow reveal of your hands,
hold out your palm to show me the well-shaped ice,
now transformed by your alchemy, to a diamond in the raw.

To Sir with love

Helen Curtis

a whiff of the lab
from his sag-hemmed jacket,
flowers of sulphur -
he is home;

long ago,
we cast aside titration, calculation
and tweezered crystals into waterglass
and watched

cobalt, nickel, chrome
blossom into globules, pinnacles,
inflorescence of lapis,
brimstone.

and still years on
his rough tweed brushes
tints into the air
and colours me in.

Safe Sex

MJ Oliver

www.youtu.be/uZJJ2dotayl

We adored those randy forks-of-lightning
that struck at random on the kitchen-table

and were bewildered in our old age
when they ceased.

It took years – and ping-pong –
for-us to find each-other-again.

A green net's now stretched across the table,
witness to a brand new yin-and-yang.

Striving for perfection, north south, east west,
north north-east, we're laughing

from-the-floor at failed shots, spinning
with-joy when the jackpot's-hit, cheeks-pink

as peonies, as the rising-dipping orange ball
sizzles between-us.

Short Stories

The short story category was for entries of up to 2,000 words, not including the title. The short story genre is a staple of writing competitions the world over and many writers will hone their skills in this medium before venturing into the world of longer fiction.

In some ways, writing short fiction is much harder than writing longer pieces, this is because the writer doesn't have the luxury of space and time to expand on a theme or introduce too many layers. Most short stories seem to work best when they consider a single perspective or a specific event.

Advice from our Short Story judges

Ginna Wilkerson

www.ginnawilkerson.weebly.com

As we all know, writers are always readers first. My best advice is to read as much as you can of the genre you wish to write. Think about which pieces catch your attention and hold it straight through to the ending. Also notice the pieces that you did not enjoy as much. Why? Was it difficult to follow? Maybe the author changed POV or verb tense. Did you not understand the characters? Maybe the author didn't take time to develop them before telling the story. Ask all the questions. Then remember the four qualities of all outstanding prose writing, whether fiction or non-fiction: organization, support, unity, and coherence. And, finally, remember to proof-read before submitting!

Sal Page

sal-cobbledtogether.blogspot.co.uk

Start further into the story than you want to, or remove those initial paragraphs after the first draft. Get straight into the action. Anything important can be implied later. Don't tell the reader someone is the husband or the daughter, show us through dialogue and action.

Try to avoid massive chunks of back story. Feed in just enough to keep the reader intrigued and guessing. It's surprising how much can be hidden in the sub text.

If you write your story in second person you must have a really good reason for doing so.

We're often told not to write from the point of view of a child, animal or inanimate object. I think its fine you just have to make it work.

Be careful describing a person when in their close point of view. They can't see themselves. We don't think about the colour of our hair or eyes. An elderly person will not consider their wrinkles or the way they walk while events are unfolding. A large person will not think of themselves as 'lumbering'.

Read your dialogue in particular out loud. Folk are more likely to say 'don't' than 'do not', 'can't' than 'cannot', rarely use 'however' or 'nevertheless' in conversation and will often leave out the 'I' when talking of themselves.

The best stories I read while judging this competition weren't just well written; they left me getting what the writer was trying to say and thinking about the character(s) and their situation afterwards. They had a satisfying completeness and a purpose.

One very simple thing; do a search for the word 'that'. The majority will be superfluous and your story improved with them banished.

Above all, the reader should be so engrossed in the story they don't notice your writing, even though it's your writing that's making them engrossed.

Tamara Jones

The single aspect common of many stories in this competition that consistently lost points in my eyes, was the ending. I read a number of well written and engaging stories which were let down badly by a weak or confusing ending. I came away feeling disappointed, let down, cheated, sometimes quite sad that what should have been a good involving story petered out into pointlessness because of its highly unsatisfying ending. For me, the end is probably the most important

49

part of the story, it's the bit that keeps the story alive in my mind after finishing, so perhaps a useful technique to ensuring the ending is strong and memorable (thus making the story likewise) would be to start with the end and work backwards. Not easy and not always desirable, but worth doing if only to get a sense of how well - or not - the ending works.

Lucy Williams

Beware of overwriting. I have read so many exciting stories with characters that I was immediately drawn to, which then left me hugely dissatisfied when the writer starts adding far too much information, stating the obvious and putting me off reading more. It's such a shame when that happens because with some stripping back they could be really compelling pieces of work. Often the piece could have ended a few paragraphs back, for instance. I was once advised to go back to what you think is a finished story and chop the first 3 lines, and last 3 lines, just to see if it still stands. If it does then you know you need to have a bit of an edit.

Try to add some small details here and there about your characters so that you evoke them a little more clearly for the reader. Often I read a fantastic story with a really interesting character but found myself completely unable to picture the character at all, or to place their age, style, etc. Just a small, subtle detail about clothing or appearance can do wonders for the reader.

Read a handful of short stories, then the following day make a note of which ones you remember. Ask yourself what it is you remember about them. How did they reach out to you, shake you up, and leave you changed? Imagine that you had to judge them all. What order would you place them in and why. Take the time to do it and you will hopefully think differently.

As challenging as the short story can be, enjoy its ability to cover small subjects. Think of something seemingly small in everyday life and explore it from a new perspective. Write a whole story about something you have never read about before. Look in your own journals. Shine a light on a little corner of your life for us.

Ayalla Buchanan

My most important advice would be to read and follow the instructions, don't get yourself disqualified because you didn't include something that was required.

No Odysseus

Shauna Mackay

Belter Brenda wants Malc and Malc wants Belter Brenda, only trouble is Malc's got the wife and bairn at home. 'See this,' he says to the lads, and he raises his ring finger, 'I don't wear this thing for fun.'

'Nobody's said nowt,' says Dobbs.

Malc takes a good swallow of his pint. 'You know Odysseus, right?'

'Eh?' says Tommo.

'I've heard of the bloke,' says Dobbs. 'How you so up on him, like?'

'I did learn something at school, you know, Dobbs. He's the one who had a right time of it getting back from the Trojan War. Hell of a sea voyage that lad had to contend with.' Malc's gaze strays from his two mates' ugly mugs and travels the length of the Memorial Hall to where Brenda's taking to the stage. She's got her shiny red dress on and he has to close his eyes against her curves.

'Are you thinking you might do off to sea yourself, like?' cracks Dobbs. 'If the redundancy rumours turn out to be true?'

All three of them work on the bins. Dobbs and Tommo have always been there for Malc. Fantastic they were last year when he wasn't himself for a bit after the bairn got diagnosed with the CF. Cystic Fibrosis it stands for and it means Malc and the wife have to slap the poor little bugger's body about everyday so his lungs don't get all clogged up. Coughs like an auld pitman. Malc wishes CF was transferable. He'd like to take it from the bairn. If only he could.

'Earth calling Malc,' says Tommo.

'Sorry,' says Malc.

'What's the big deal with this Odysseus, then?' Dobbs asks him. 'Make it sharpish though. Brenda's doing her one twos.'

'Well,' says Malc, and then he stops because he spots his mother-in-law's sister sitting a couple of tables away. 'Put your backs together, lads,' he says, all stiff-lipped like a ventriloquist.

The lads look around and spot bat ears. 'Aw, I catch your drift,' says Tommo, and he shuffles in his stool to make a pow-wow.

'She's all lugs that one,' says Dobbs. 'She'll have her hearing aid amped up to the hilt. Probably a lip-reader. Wouldn't put it past her. Auld gossip. Got a bloody nerve when her Patsy's the village bike.'

'Don't,' says Malc.

'It's true,' says Dobbs.

'Luckily for you, Dobbs,' says Tommo.

'Listen, lads, it's like this, right, I don't know how much longer I can keep Brenda at bay.' Malc has a quick drink of his pint. 'She's coming on strong.'

'Aw, I really feel for you,' says Tommo.

'It's not funny,' says Malc.

'What's this Odysseus bloke got to do with the price of fish?' asks Dobbs.

'He had his mates tie him to a pole so he could hear the sirens' song without coming a cropper.'

'I've always said you're a bit touched, Malc,' says Tommo.

'The sirens, right,' says Malc, 'they were these seductive women, well they were half women, half bird, following so far?'

'Which half was the bird half?' says Tommo.

'What way round do you reckon would be best, Tommo?' says Dobbs.

'This is serious stuff,' says Malc. Sometimes he knows what it is to be all at sea even though the only time he's ever been on a boat was when he took the wife and bairn on that trip over to the Farne Islands to see the puffins. That was the week after they found out about the CF. It had been a rough crossing but the three of them had laughed all the way over. Coming back, the sea had settled itself down. 'The sirens used to sing and lure sailors to their death,' he says now, almost past caring.

'What did they sing? Chirpy Chirpy Cheep Cheep?' says Dobbs.

'By, you're going back a bit there, lad,' says Tommo. 'I know you're as auld as the hills, like, but bloody hell.'

'Are you two listening, or what?'

'Aye,' says Dobbs. 'Carry on.'

'Most sailors would do anything not to hear the sirens' song, right? Because they know it's curtains if they do. Not Odysseus though.'

'What did Oddsy do, then?' Dobbs shrugs at Malc and Tommo. 'That's what we'd call him if he was on the bins with us.'

'He's just said, Dobbs. He had his mates tie him to a pole.'

'He wanted to hear the song but not succumb,' says Malc. 'And that's what I'm going to do with the help of you two bonny lads.'

'You want me and Tommo to tie you to a pole?'

'It can be easily arranged,' says Tommo.

'Not an actual pole,' says Malc. 'A metaphorical one.'

'A whattie?' says Tommo.

'Look,' says Malc, 'I could easily stop indoors with the wife of a Saturday night, away from Belter Brenda and her come ons but I want the night out, don't I? I like the banter with you two jokers and I enjoy a pint or six. Do you know what I'm saying?'

'I think so,' says Dobbs.

'I'm not sure,' says Tommo.

'I'm going to do an Odysseus. I'm going to hear Brenda sing. When she holds those top notes I'm going to watch her boobs tremble like two frightened doves huddled together for comfort and later on when they call time at the bar and she's giving me the glad eye, you two are going to hold me back. But there's no actual pole, you both got that?'

'I think I've got the gist of it,' says Tommo.

'Clear as mustard,' says Dobbs, stretching his neck up so he can see the stage better where Brenda's singing about setting fire to the rain.

'Is that a figure or is that a figure?' says Dobbs.

'That's a figure,' says Tommo.

Brenda looks like a goddess tonight. Malc wonders how it would feel to be all over her naked body. Lost to the redundancy rumours, lost to the fact the bairn's got the CF, lost to everything but Brenda's warm flesh. There's a key change now and the song soars and Malc thinks about the two doves being released. Waves of wanting crash onto the shore of his shoes, white horses gallop up his trousers, trample his chest only to be brought up short, panting at his head. He'a a married man. He made vows in front of a vicar. Half the village was there and God was likely watching. Brenda and him can't happen. He's done the right thing in enlisting the lads to the cause. She's a temptation he needs help with.

Come last orders and Brenda's bothering him. She's pushed up behind him at the bar, pressing her hands over his eyes. 'Guess who? She says, her sticky breath warms his right ear.

'It's Dobbs, isn't it?' he says. 'I'd recognise those soft hands anywhere.'

She laughs and sidles in beside him. Malc girds himself with the thought the lads are on standby and, bonus fact, his mother-in-law's sister's looking sozzled and won't remember her own name tomorrow never mind that Brenda has squeezed up to Malc at closing time.

'Warm, isn't it?' says Brenda.

'Very,' he says. 'Can I get you a drink?'

'I'll have a pint of cider and black, ta.'

He orders the drinks and they smile at each other. She's got a load of teeth but she's not at all horsey, thinks Malc. And some might call her fat but he'd call her fit. God, she is fit alright. He likes a woman with a bit of meat on. 'Smashing show you put on tonight, Brenda.' He looks over her head to try and catch one of the lads' eyes but Tommo's not there and Dobbs is too busy acting the goat with Patsy.

'Something up, Malc?' says Brenda.

'No,' he says, trying not to show he's ruffled as hell. The barmaid's finished pulling the three Fosters and Brenda's already lifted her cider and black to her lips. He digs into his pocket for his last note.

'Cheers,' she says. 'I hope you're not going to leave me to sip this on my lonesome?'

'Er, well, you know, the lads are waiting, like.'

She gets jostled by Franky Pledger who's in a rush to get a last drink in and her chest gets pressed up against Malc. Her eyes are a dare. 'Go give those two their drinks and get yourself back,' she tells him.

He picks up two pints. 'Excuse me,' he says, and he shoulders his way through the crowd.

Dobbs is being straddled by Patsy. 'Where's Tommo?' Malc asks him.

'Had to leg it or he was going to miss the chippy.'

'I'll chippy him,' says Malc. He glances back over at Brenda. She's watching him and waves. 'Patsy, love, go and powder your nose or something, I need a little word with my pal here.'

'Who do you think you are?' says Patsy.

'I'm a desperate man, Patsy, that's who I am. I'm Mr bloody Desperate of Desperateville, now please have a heart and give Dobbs and me a private minute here.'

Patsy flings her round blue eyes up to the roof of the Memorial Hall but then she jumps up off Dobbs and leaves.

'You're needy these days, lad,' says Dobbs.

Malc puts the pints down. 'What happened to our pact?' Dobbs twists up his eye, trying to figure out what Malc's going on about. Malc helps him out. 'The pole thing? Brenda's nearly eaten me alive over there. Fat lot of good you are.' Dobbs is looking to see where Patsy's gone. What's the bloody point? Thinks Malc. 'Look, I'm going to get off home now.'

'Sensible lad,' says Dobbs. 'I'm going to Patsy's party.'

'How old are you, Dobbs?' Malc shakes his head. 'Do you not think it's time to give Patsy's parties a swerve? Time to grow up. You're baldy and you've got an enlarged prostate.'

Dobbs winks and clicks his mouth. 'Peter Pan,' he says. 'Anyway, Malc, you get yourself back up that hillside to your little cottage and your lovely little family and Belter Brenda will just have to find some other lucky sod to seduce. Tell her I'm up for it, if you like?'

'See you Monday,' says Malc. 'Thanks for nowt.'

'No bother, mate,' says Dobbs.

Malc grabs his jacket from the back of the chair, ducks his head down, and leaves.

He's not two minutes up the road when he hears his name being called. It's only bloody Brenda. He turns and she starts running toward him and all he can think about is the glistening in the dark. It's from her red sequins and the rain. Everything's all wet with silvery rain.

'Hoy there, handsome, what's your hurry?'

'I have to get home.'

'Oh, come to mine and have a coffee or something,' she says. 'I left the heating on. Get yourself warmed up before you head for the hills.'

'I can't,' he says. He's not looking at her because he can't look at her. He's never fancied anyone as much as he fancies her at this moment. 'I'm sorry,' he says.

'Come on,' she says, and she grabs his hand. 'We're all sorry.'

She lives in the high street above the candle shop. They've already kissed twice and she's looking in her handbag for her key when his phone goes. It's the wife. The bairn isn't well. He's had Calpol and she's let him have his dummy, but he's still not settling. He wants his dad.

Malc double checks he's turned his phone off and then he says, 'this is not happening, not tonight, not any night, never. I'm a married man.'

She strokes his cheek. 'You are,' she says.

Malc turns from her and starts out again, at speed. He knows he's no Odysseus but he does know how it feels to want nothing but home. It feels like this.

Colony

Victoria Briggs

motherpussbucket.wordpress.com

The first ant was an outrider. Alone in the bedroom, antennae waving, searching for food on the pale tiled floor. Maxine spotted it the second she went in there with her suitcase.

George heard the squeal and arrived in the bedroom just as Maxine was kicking off her flip-flop. The first slap alone was enough to do the job, but she continued smacking the floor with increasing fervour.

'Disgusting. Ring reception, George. Tell them we want another room.'

'We're in a ground floor apartment, babe. It's probably just wandered in from the outside.'

'I don't want to sleep in the same room as ants. They'll be crawling all over us in the night, biting.'

George looked at his watch. 'I thought you wanted to catch some sun before dinner? If we have to switch apartments, we're going to miss the last of the day.'

Maxine dropped the flip-flop and rose from her executioner's position on the floor. They'd had a terrible journey to the island – their flight had been delayed. She looked at the ant stain on the floor; it was the last straw.

'I want an upgrade for this. One of those rooms with a view that we saw in the brochure.'

George pretended not to hear. Once Maxine got an idea in her head, it was hard to shake her free of it. A single thought could end up possessing her for weeks.

'You go and relax by the pool,' he said. 'It's been a long day.'

Maxine wandered off into the bathroom, still talking about upgrades through a half closed door. George didn't fancy their chances when it came to persuading the manager of a better room: it was high season, the hotel was full and a single ant didn't give them much in the way of bargaining power.

He thought the apartment was decent enough considering it had been a late booking. It was on a self-catering complex in a quiet resort. George wandered around getting the feel of the place. There was a kitchen and a dining area. There was even some outside space – a small patio with a garden.

From behind the bathroom door, George heard the snap of a bikini clasp then Maxine appeared in a hot pink two-piece, announcing her arrival with a theatrical, 'da-dah.'

George wasn't much of a sunbather. His skin was the kind that reddened and turned prickly in the heat. His temperament reacted in much the same way. He preferred his own company, reading a novel in the shade, over forced conversations with half naked strangers crowded round a pool.

'You go for a dip,' he said. 'I'll check to make sure there aren't any more ants.'

When she'd left, George went out on the patio to continue his inspection of the property. Theirs was a corner apartment. Vivid blooms of Bougainvillea climbed the whitewashed walls and a sea-salt breeze blew in from the west. He sat down in a garden chair and studied the flagged floor. There was no sign of any ants.

George wondered whether to unpack or not. He felt sure there was no point in putting it off – there was only a remote chance of the manager giving them another apartment – but to assume defeat before they'd even asked was to risk Maxine's ire for the rest of their stay.

He needn't have worried. 'It's beautiful out there,' said Maxine when she returned, all memory of ant and upgrade erased by the sun.

Next morning, Maxine left the apartment early in pursuit of a prime sun bed while George opted for a lie in. It was some time later when he was eating breakfast out on the patio that the first crumb fell: a flake of golden croissant with a smudge of strawberry jam.

Somewhere beneath the flagstones, the smell of sugar crystals makes a small ant swoon.

George had just opened the first page of his book when he saw a dark fleck moving out the corner of his eye. He put his book down on the table and bent forwards, assuming an ant's eye view – the flagstones becoming a vast and barren plain; the crumb of croissant, some fallen manna from a pink-skinned god.

'Hello there,' said George to the ant and then, remembering that all worker ants were female, he added: 'I'm sorry about your sister.'

He watched the ant waving its antennae, reading pheromones on the breeze. He wondered what signals it was picking up. What news of its discovery was it sending home?

Just then, another ant climbed up between the flagstones, zig-zagging its way across the concrete, compelled towards the golden crumb.

Soon the pair were joined by more ants. By the time a small clan had gathered, George had forgotten all about his book. He had forgotten too about Maxine's reaction to the bedroom ant the day before. Using the tip of his little finger, he swept up the remnants of croissant from his breakfast plate and flicked them towards the floor.

'For your queen,' he said.

It was almost lunchtime when Maxine returned to the flat. The sun had hit its high point in the sky, bleaching the day in a glare of brilliant white. George had spent the whole morning on the patio watching the ants heave and carry the pastry flakes home.

When he heard Maxine's key turn in the lock, he jumped to his feet knocking his chair backwards in surprise.

'Don't tell me you've been in bed all morning,' she called out.

George burst into the apartment, locking the patio door behind him and pulling down the blinds. 'I lost track of time,' he said.

'Are you hungry? We could eat at one of those cafés near the beach.'

'The beach! What a good idea,' George said, pushing his feet into some sandals and walking Maxine back in the direction of the door.

At the café, George ordered lunch: more food than they could eat, a large carafe of wine, then a drawn out dessert of ice cream and fruit. Afterwards he insisted on a walk back to the apartment via the long way round, past the fishing boats in the cove, past the lighthouse, to the tip of the rocky headland. They stopped for photos, then more photos, until Maxine complained that she needed a pee and he had no choice but to head back to the apartment. They'd been gone almost three full hours by then. Time enough, he hoped, for the ants to remove all trace of their existence.

The rest of the week settled into a similar routine. Maxine would leave the apartment before breakfast to secure a sun bed, marking her territory with an oversized beach towel and reserving two more for her new friends, Marco and Gianni.

George spent his mornings with the colony. 'Good morning, ladies,' he called towards the flagstones at the start of every day, his voice sinking down between the cracks. Within a minute, the ants would come to greet him, two at a time, their mandibles out-stretched before them.

'Toast and marmalade on the menu,' he'd say, or else, 'It's boiled egg and soldiers today.'

He liked to vary their diet, working in a little protein, although they, like he, had an insatiable sweet tooth.

'We'll try some sausage tomorrow, shall we? On white bread with ketchup.'

Maybe it was because he was leaving down bigger pieces of food, but more ants seemed to gather every day. George enjoyed testing their resourcefulness. Using chocolate-chip cookies broken into chunks, he would coax them into increasing displays of industry and strength.

To his surprise, Maxine didn't seem to mind his pool-side absences. He blamed it on his book, how engrossed he was in the plot. Maxine had shrugged. Through the apartment window, he could see her splashing about in the pool with Marco, Gianni and some woman in a string bikini. A volleyball match was underway. It seemed the four of them had paired into teams of mixed doubles.

George disliked team sports. He was not competitive by nature. Neither were the ants, who built and busied and worked together for the colony's good.

Out on the patio, he extended his foot across the flagstone until he felt the soft probe of an ant's antennae against his little toe, smelling him, tasting.

'Too salty for you?' he asked as it climbed down off his foot and retraced its steps back towards the cookie chunk.

On the last day of the holiday, George offered to spend the morning packing so Maxine could have a final dip in the pool. After seven days in the sun, she was the colour of toasted almonds.

'You look good enough to eat, babe,' he told her.

'We should have booked for two weeks, George. I'm only just starting to relax.'

George didn't disagree. He too would have liked more time here before they headed home. He had begun to think about the ants' winter stocks – would they have enough food to see them through till spring time? Who would be the next residents in their apartment? If they weren't as concerned as he about the ants' feeding regime, it was easy to imagine they might run short.

The coach to take them to the airport was due at noon. After he finished packing, George washed their coffee cups in the kitchen sink and watched Maxine from the window. She was by the pool, rubbing sun lotion into Marco's back.

George left time before the coach came to have one last breakfast with the ants. Today was a special occasion. He'd been down to the local shop and bought an ice-glazed doughnut. The ants would think it was Christmas, and George could rest easy knowing their sugar supply was assured.

Out on the patio he broke the doughnut into pieces and scattered them in the undergrowth, out of range of the cleaner's mop and bucket. He'd only just camouflaged the last piece beneath some twigs when Maxine appeared.

'What are you doing?'

George was sat on his haunches. The palms of his hands were covered in soil.

'Nothing,' he said, wiping his hands down his t-shirt before adding, 'I thought I dropped something.'

'Well don't just sit there. The coach will be here soon.'

George got to his feet and went to gather his things from the table. Maxine was on her way in when she turned round to say something and stopped. A vast dark army was swarming up between the flagstones. Maxine stared at the ground and pointed, backing slowly towards the apartment.

'George,' she said. 'Call the manager.'

'It's alright, babe,' he said, attempting to guide her through the patio doors.

'Call the manager. Quickly, before they get in.'

'I'll have a word as we're checking out. Now, let's just get you back inside.'

Maxine pulled away from him and ran into the apartment. She headed for the kitchen, diving into a cupboard beneath the sink where the cleaning products were stored.

'I told you we should have got another apartment,' she shouted. 'The whole place is infested.'

George stood by the patio doors, helpless, while she ran out into the garden, emptying a bottle of disinfectant over the teeming flagstones. He knew he should do something but didn't know what. When he did spring into action, making a late grab for the disinfectant bottle, he ended up spattering the last of its contents down both of their legs.

On the drive to the airport George sat in an aisle seat, his eyes trained down the centre of the coach, staring blankly at the road ahead. Maxine was dabbing at her sandals with a tissue. The disinfectant stains had soaked into the leather turning them a greasy shade of brown.

'They're ruined, George. Totally ruined.'

George nodded in agreement, his eyes fixed on the road. The disinfectant smell still filling his airways so that he could taste it on his tongue.

The Waitress's Confession

Lucy Welsh

www.lucywelch.tk

Bacon fat and coffee. Those smells will follow me to my grave, I reckon. I'm not complaining though: in a funny sort of way, I've probably had some of my happiest times working shifts in this greasy spoon cafe.

I've got my regulars. See that guy in the corner, with the grey in his beard? Looks like he should be a sailor about to set out to sea, don't you think? He's really a bus driver, comes in every morning for a fry up before he starts his route. There's a few more like him, you get to know them after a while. They're like me, we've all got the same look in our eyes, that look you get when know you've screwed up your chances and you've just got to get on with it the best you can. Oh yes, they could tell a story or two.

But it's not their stories I'm telling today. No, I want to make a confession of my own. Don't roll your eyes like that; I need to tell someone, so why not you?

See that table in the corner, right near the kitchen door? For weeks and weeks the same girl used to come and have her breakfast right there, pile of books at her elbow, listening to music on her IPod. Lovely looking girl; gorgeous blonde hair and a serious look about her, like she was going to make a difference in her life. And you'd never have thought she could put away scrambled eggs and bacon like she did every morning - there wasn't a scrap of fat on her. She'd have caught your eye, if you'd seen her, and you wouldn't have been the only one.

A young man started coming in at the same time, and he'd always find a place at one of the tables near her and sit and stare over his coffee.

Fabulous eyes he had, moody grey and shining like when the sun catches the bottom of a thundercloud, you know what I mean? They made me think of another pair of eyes, just like that, which I fell in love with a long time ago. Perhaps that's what made me say it. Remembering those wonderful eyes.

"Go and ask her out," I told him. I'd gone to fill his coffee cup - that's what keeps the punters coming back here, you know, the coffee refills. He looked up, startled like, those beautiful eyes all soft and dreamy and I told him again - "Ask her out! She's a lovely girl, she won't bite."

I suppose I was feeling quite soppy, remembering, and that's why I leant in and whispered over the coffee pot in my hand.

"That's how I met my fella," I told him, "all those years ago. He saw me in a cafe and came over to ask me out."

He asked, "And you said yes, just like that?"

"See," I said. "It's not so hard. That cup of tea began the best years of my life. Imagine if he'd never dared ask!"

But he must have seen regret pulling lines down my face because he asked, "What happened?"

What happened? Sally happened, that's what I wanted to tell him. With her long legs and short skirts and that stupid little pout that she did. I wasn't even surprised when my fella admitted that he'd strayed. Just the once, he swore with his hand on his heart when he begged me to forgive him. Lord knows, I wish I had but back then I was young and didn't know that life doesn't often give second chances.

So when I opened my mouth to try and explain to the boy where it all went wrong, the truth fell out. "I ran away," I said. "I ran from him and I ran from my poor baby, Lord forgive me."

Well, that made him sit up straight. "Baby?"

Then I recollected myself. A quick glance round showed a dozen heads turned in my direction, trying to get my attention, and Fat Bill was tinging the bell in the kitchen like there were a hundred breakfasts waiting to get onto tables.

"Never you mind," I told the boy hastily. "Just ask her out!"

I was run off my feet for the next hour so I didn't have room in my head for the memories that kept trying to barge their way in. But I did see the boy get up and go to her table. Not that he was really a boy any more: his legs were still long and gawky like a teenagers but his shoulders were filling out so you could see the man he would become. She gave him a smile like summer sunshine and then she pushed over a chair so he could join her and they sat there, chatting away over cold coffee for ages. I kept glancing over, feeling warm inside like I'd done a good thing, then one time I looked and they were gone.

I didn't see either of them for a week or two. That's that, I thought, with an odd sort of pride that they were getting on with their lives but sad at the same time, like I'd bought myself a ticket to the cinema and was watching lives being lived out instead of living my own.

And he'd kicked up a swarm of memories, that boy with the bright, stormy eyes. Scraps of times long ago whirled in my head like bees, the good times and the bad, and the one that stung the most was the day when I'd gone back to find my fella. Crept back, I should say, with an apology on my lips and a candle of hope in my eyes but I never spoke to him. I was waiting in the street when I saw him coming with Sally, both of them laughing in that special way so that I knew, I just knew. And the little boy toddling between them, both of them holding one of his hands and swinging him up in the air so that he shrieked with glee. Too late for me.

So I left them alone. Walking away was like slamming a knife in my gut and I cried for my fella and my sweet baby, every night for years. But crying never changes a thing and that's the truth.

And there I was, pouring coffee and serving breakfasts, chatting to my regulars while I tried to forget my own screw ups and hoping that the boy would make a better job of life with that lovely girl, when, lo and behold, the pair of them walked back in. They didn't go to her old table but headed straight for the counter, looking in my direction with odd, set looks on their faces.

The girl was a step ahead, the boy lagging reluctantly as if she pulled him along on an invisible leash. So I smiled at her and said, "Scrambled eggs and bacon?"

She shook her head, as serenely solemn as an angel at a deathbed, she was. But then the young think everything's either hilarious or terribly serious so I wasn't worried.

"We came to talk to you," she said.

"You don't have to thank me," I said brightly. "Anyone could see you were made for each other."

She shook her head and fired an urgent look at the boy, who dragged his feet up to the counter. His eyes were full of rainclouds.

"Tell her," said the girl.

He looked at me without saying a word until I said, all puzzled like, "Tell me what?"

"You were wrong," he said. "I was plucking up the nerve to speak to someone, but it wasn't her."

He offered his girlfriend an apologetic look but she just nodded, urging him on.

72

He turned his luminescent eyes back on me and I thought - God doesn't give those eyes to just anyone. Then I knew, in a quiet, surprised sort of way like I'd known the first minute I saw him and just hadn't been able to admit it until right then.

He pushed something over the counter and I looked down, glad to hide my tears. It was a happy family photo, radiant with that new-parent smile, you know the one, proud and exhausted and full of awe at what you've done. A man with his arm round his girl as she cradles a baby.

"That's you in the photo, isn't it?" he said.

I don't remember ever being so fresh and hopeful as the girl in that photo but she still looked like me somehow.

"It was so long ago," I said.

"You and my father." Before I could ask he said flatly, "He died last year. Cancer. And, well it's a long story but I fell out with my mother and I'm never speaking to her again."

I tell you, I was just staring at that photo like I hoped I could tumble right in and live it out a different way. But I had to ask.

"Your mother's name is Sally?"

He leant in close and I could tell he was willing me to look up. "They told me she was my mother. But it isn't true, is it? He always loved you more, you know. He never got over you leaving.

And when I found this photo I worked it out. That's me in the photo, isn't it?" As quick as a whip he flipped over the photo to show big black numbers in a confident hand - nineteen ninety five. "That's the year I was born," he said, like it proved everything.

Thing is, a lot happened that year. I wish I could just remember the milky smell of my little boy or his newborn fingers wrapped round mine. But when I look back I see the black hole in the ground and the tiny white casket. I'll never forget how angry I was that Sally came to the church, her black funeral dress stretched over her swollen belly and with such a smug look that I could have smashed my fist in her face. The injustice of it all! I remember my fella trying to put his arms round me, trying to comfort me, but I wouldn't let him. Not when everyone could see what he'd done. It's not like infidelity causes cot death, is it? But it sure felt like it.

So, I finally looked up and opened my mouth to tell the kid to go home to his mother. But those eyes, those wonderful eyes, hopefully bright like the sun shining through morning mist. Just like his father's eyes all those years ago! Can you really say you'd have done different? When life seems to tip the scales of justice your way, you don't mess it up a second time!

"My beautiful boy," I said, looking straight into those eyes. "I thought about you every single day."

Feed Me

Alexandra Swinburn

Abruptly, in the middle of the night, he came into her room.

'Gloria, are you sleeping?' A pause. 'Gloria?'

Slowly, she opened her eyes a fraction to squint through the darkness. 'I was,' she mumbled dully. 'But I'm not now,'

'Sorry. Did I wake you?'

A sigh of sour breath slipped from her lips. 'You always do. What do you want, Gordon?'

'Oh you know... Just a chat,'

A chat. A chat about nothing. Or nothing she would want to hear. She rolled over onto her other side and covered her face with the spare pillow. 'I'm going back to sleep now,' she mumbled, but he did not go away.

'We always used to have such good chats before,'

'Gordon, for God's sakes.'

He was quiet then. She could hear him thinking, dredging up old memories like pulling pebbles from the bottom of a muddy pond. Things she did not want to remember, that she had tried hard to forget. Not that he would let her.

'I remember you in your little nightie,'

'Gordon-,'

'It barely covered your lovely arse,'

Her eyes flew open again. 'It's the middle of the bloody night! I need my sleep!'

'I miss that nightie. I miss those days,'

'Well I don't. So leave me alone,'

He could not be so easily dissuaded. 'I was thinking about our first time in Florida,' he said. 'I burnt my scalp to a crisp and you broke your big toe falling out of the taxi. Remember that, sweetheart?'

Her wristwatch said 2:52 a.m. She scowled and threw the pillow across the room. 'Do we have to do this now?' There was a sigh, a pause, but it wasn't over yet.

'The hotel was superb,' he continued. 'I can't remember a better one. Lovely meals we had there, too. All that fish, excellent barbecues, and the most enormous desserts.'

He chuckled. She stared out at the darkness. Oh no, Gloria thought, her stomach clenching. Here it comes.

'You know how I like my puddings. Cream cakes, tarts and pastries... I could eat my own weight in sweets. I could do that every day. I could-,'

'Stop it! Just stop!' She sat up sharply and flung her hands up to the sides of her head. 'I can't take this, Gordon, I just can't!'

The tears came then, sudden and unstoppable. Gloria sobbed, giving way to her wretched frustration at last. Why couldn't he just bugger off? Why did he have to keep on? He knew she was desperate to lose weight. Fifty-two years old and twenty-three stones: she felt and looked ancient and enormous. And he, king of the blubber belly, built like a bloody great walrus, was doing nothing, nothing, to help.

76

'I can't keep doing this, Gordon,' she cried. 'You know you'll end up killing me with this damned fixation of yours.'

Silence. Her tears made him uncomfortable, at least for a while. Gloria sobbed until she had no more energy to continue, and then she sat, breathing heavily, staring at the outline of her fat shape beneath the quilt.

Gently, Gordon suggested, 'Maybe you should have a cup of tea. It might make you feel better.'

Gloria nodded. She swung her heavy legs over the side of the bed and threw off the covers. In the darkness her toes found her slippers and she shuffled out, onto the landing, past the bathroom and the guest room, and then down the stairs. The hallway was cold, and she shivered as she walked through the dining room and into the kitchen.

Darkness. Outside the streetlights were off. She stood at the sink, filling the kettle, staring out at the silent neighbourhood. All those people, snugly sound asleep, not awake and troubled like she was. Gordon's car sat on the driveway. He hadn't driven it in ages but he wouldn't let her sell it. Typical of him, she scowled; he just couldn't let go of things, even when he had no choice.

The tea did not make her feel better, not at all. She told him so when he came down and hovered at her shoulder.

'Maybe your blood sugar's low,' he told her as she sat at the table. 'Have a biscuit or two, that'll cheer you up,'

'I shouldn't be eating in the middle of the night,'

Gordon snorted disdainfully. 'Did those Slimmer's World harpies tell you that? It's a lie, old girl. I bet if you asked them if you could eat one of their ludicrously-priced chocolate bars at three in the morning, they'd think that was fine. More profit for them! Go on, there are some chocolate digestives in the barrel.'

'Don't call me old girl,' Gloria snapped. But she was already reaching for the biscuits, and before she knew it the taste of chocolate was in her mouth.

He was right, though she didn't tell him so: the biscuit did bring her comfort. As did the second, the third and the fourth. But the empty packet made her angry again.

'Look what you made me do!' she railed at him, throwing the packet across the room. 'That's over five hundred calories, right there, all before breakfast!'

'Now don't get upset,' Gordon said. 'It's just a sugar rush,'

She struggled up from her chair. 'I am upset,' she snapped. 'What kind of husband does this to his wife? I mean, look at me.' She waved her thick arms and through the darkness peered down at herself. 'I'm a whale. And it's all your fault, you know that don't you? If you weren't so obsessed with food and sweets, I'd be half the size! And if I was half the size, I'd be off tomorrow, looking for another man. I'd leave this place in a heartbeat, do you know that? You could take this house and everything in it and shove it!'

He was shocked. 'Don't say that,' he said, voice trembling. 'All I ever wanted was for you to be happy,'

Gloria's face was puce with anger. 'Well I'm not happy, Gordon. I haven't been happy for a very long time. Not that you ever cared enough to notice.'

There was a long pause, a heavy, painful silence. After enduring it for as long as she could, Gloria bent down and retrieved the empty biscuit packet. She was just about to drop it into the bin when she heard him say,

'You can't leave me. I won't let you do that. I just won't.'

Instantly her blood froze. So, that was it. He'd laid his cards out at last. She would never have any peace, not a chance to lose all that awful weight and get back to how she once was. He'd keep on pushing her, encouraging her to eat all those sweet, calorific foods, and eventually it would be the death of her.

Something snapped inside Gloria then. She could not let this go on. It was abuse, plain and simple, and it had to stop.

She straightened up, fist clenching around the empty wrapper, and slowly turned around.

'So that's how it is,' she whispered, more to herself than to her husband. 'Well, if that's how you want it, Gordon.'

He said nothing as she shuffled towards the fridge and opened the door, sending a triangle of pale light across the kitchen. Inside, the shelves groaned. She'd gone shopping only yesterday. Full-fat yoghurts, milk and cream. A family-sized apple pie. Chocolate cake. Chicken pizza. Barbecue ribs. Bacon, cheeses and ready-made lasagne. To say nothing of the four tubs of ice-cream and the strawberry gateau stuffed inside the freezer.

Gloria started with the milk. She opened the carton, tipped her head back and drank a third of it. Voluptuously creamy. Then the apple pie. It was stodgy and over-sweet but she didn't care. She ate it with her fingers, pulling off chunks and swallowing it quickly. Behind her, Gordon gave a shriek of delight.

'Oh, that looks delicious!' he cried. 'How's the cake? Try it, Gloria, try it,'

She did as he asked, unwrapping the box and sinking her hands into the dark, sticky mass. It stuck to her face as she ate, but she didn't care how much mess she made.

'Good? Is it?'

He was at her shoulder again. She could feel the weight of him, all excited and energized. Nodding, she kept on eating.

'That's it, old girl. Try everything, for me.'

Gloria obeyed. Sweet, savoury, cooked and raw, she devoured it all, eating until her jaws ached and the tears had begun to run down her face again. Syrup and sauces dribbled down her chin and onto her nightgown. She sank to her knees, and with Gordon urging her on continued to eat, ignoring how much her heart was racing, how distended her stomach was becoming. Just when she thought it must surely burst, she felt a fluttering in her gullet and realised she was about to vomit.

A torrent of undigested food would come spurting from her mouth, like a vile geyser. But Gloria wouldn't allow that. She clenched her jaws shut. She tightened her food-splattered hands into fists, and focused. Her brow and cheeks reddened with the effort. Gordon noticed.

'What is it, sweetheart?' he said, and there was a note of alarm in his voice. 'Are you alright?'

She managed to shake her head. No, she thought, I'm not alright. I'm about to die. And about bloody time, too!

Gradually the feeling of nausea passed. With unsteady hands, Gloria took a chunk of cheddar cheese out of its wrapper and sank her teeth into it.

Her husband still sounded concerned. 'You're looking a bit unwell,' he told her. 'And you're sweating. Maybe you should stop now.'

Gloria had no intention of stopping. Once again she told herself that it was all his fault. If only he'd accepted things. If only he'd left her alone. But he kept coming back, kept encouraging her gluttony. And now there was only one way to be rid of him.

A sudden tightness in her chest told her it was happening. A heart attack – at last! Her doctor had told her she was at risk, and that had been three years ago. Gloria hurried to swallow yet another mouthful of food. A sharp, constricting pain swelled out across her torso. Yes, this was it! Her hands dropped to her sides. She heard Gordon's panicked voice above her and then she slumped onto the cold kitchen floor.

At last he was beginning to understand what was going on. 'Gloria? Gloria!' He tried to rouse her, but she wouldn't move. 'You can't do this, old girl. I need you!'

Yes, he needed her. He always had. To do his washing, sort out the bills, and of course to make his meals and buy all his fattening treats. When he'd collapsed at work and died, she'd thought she'd be free, that here was a chance to smarten up her life, get fit again, be a merry, healthy widow.

Not so. Gordon had seen to that. He'd come back, and in death had been more gluttonous than ever. A greedy pig, completely insatiable for food. But his unearthly spirit couldn't gorge itself on cakes and pies and ice-cream. It could only watch Gloria eat, and try to remember how it all tasted.

Unseen, a desperate Gordon was howling and pleading for her to get up, yet she would not. Through pale and swollen lips she took a last triumphant breath. But before she succumbed and passed out of this world into the next, Gloria wondered if her husband would look the same on the Other Side; still as huge and fat and wobbly as she remembered him.

Just like a bloody great walrus.

Dressed in Black

Gwen Sayers

www.gwensayers.com/

A judge with a beard like Abraham Lincoln slammed his elbows on a wooden desk and glared at me with eyes of coal. The way I remember it is he said my marriage was dissolved for eternity.

Afterwards, I drove around Seattle for hours, sucking Hershey's Kisses, listening to Keith Jarrett, and worrying. Although I understood finality, I couldn't conceive of eternity. I figured the judge had sentenced me to aloneness forever. I bit my finger nails. Every woman I saw on the sidewalk was either pushing a baby carriage or chasing children big enough to walk. My ovaries ached.

I stopped off at the Bon Marché to buy a dress. Mannequins with no faces and perfect bodies flaunted summer wear, their hands cast at strange angles. I sifted through clothes racks, wanting to improve my image. The dress I picked was black and slinky, not cut low, but clingy over my breasts and loose over my hips.

Back home, I washed my hair and looped it to one side. I hung ropes of glass beads around my neck, bruised my lips with mulberry, and tinted my face ivory. I liked my reflection. I sprayed my neck and wrists with musk, lit a Marlboro, and locked the door behind me. Neon lights flashed colour in the car as I drove downtown to the Triangle.

The pub was dark and smoky. Leaning against the counter, one foot on the rail, was a nice-looking man drinking beer. He was lanky like my husband and, without my glasses, I could kid myself. He looked younger than me, carrot-topped and freckle-faced. I sat on the stool next to him and ordered wine. I tapped my nails on the counter. He took no notice. I turned towards him and cleared my throat. He was oblivious. I offered him a cigarette and asked for a light.

'What's your name?' I said.

'Zed,' he answered, clicking the lighter.

He didn't look at me. He inhaled deeply and streamed smoke from the corner of his mouth.

'I'm Jade,' I said.

It turned out Zed was from Utah, the third son in a Mormon family. He ran away from home, aged sixteen, when his father caught him with a bottle of Bourbon. First his dad beat Zed to near-death, then he yelled for Hell to finish the job. I had nothing special to tell. My past was suburban, barren. We drank until the room tilted and I spun into a vortex.

I woke in a place smelling of dirt and cooking fat, lying on a sofa with my dress wrapped around me like a bandage. My beads dug my cheek, pins and needles pricked my hand. I shook my arm until my fingers stopped tingling. I was alone in the room except for whatever was breathing nearby. I sat, as well as I could with a head that spat bats when I moved. The drapes were closed, but light splashed through the door from the passage. Lying by the fireplace was a black Doberman. Front legs stretched in front of him, face pointed to the wall, he twitched in his sleep.

Holding my head so it wouldn't rattle, I crept past the dog, through the door and into the passage. This led to a bathroom, bedroom, and kitchen. The bedroom door, like the others, was open and I went in. Zed lay naked on his back, mouth ajar for small snores. The morning sun polished his orange hair. I admired his body for a while, thinking about my husband who I knew now would not be my husband for eternity. Then I sat on the edge of the bed. Zed grunted, rolled over and pulled me towards him.

'Maria,' he said.

'Wrong, it's Jade.'

He opened his eyes. They were milky blue. 'Oh yes, the Triangle,' he said. 'How'd you get here?'

'No idea.'

'I'm surprised Darth didn't shout his head off.'

'Who's Darth?'

'My dog.'

'He's asleep.'

'You're lucky, because he hates strangers.'

'Does he bite?'

'Sure, he's a dog.'

Zed sunk his legs into Levi's. His hands were shaking like flags in the wind. 'Want a Bud?' he said.

I followed him to the kitchen. The sink was packed with dirty plates and pots. A row of containers stood on the windowsill, growing plants with wilting leaves. A fly buzzed on the windowpane. An empty plastic bowl notched with tooth prints lay overturned on the floor. The linoleum by the door had also been savaged. Zed opened two beers. I drank fast to sooth the broken bits in my head.

'Not much to eat,' he said, exploring a cupboard.

'Where's Maria?' I asked.

'Gone,' he said. He scratched a sore on his arm and a bead of blood sprouted.

A photo of Zed with a young woman was fixed to the fridge door with two magnetic hearts. The girl's hair fell over her shoulders, and she wore white shorts with a halter top. She was exquisite.

'Is this her?'

'Yes,' he said. 'She's my wife.'

'When did she leave?'

'Six months ago, maybe more.'

'Why did she go?'

'I don't know. I drank some. I got mean.' A muscle below his eye shuddered. 'Why ask these questions? You sound like the cops.'

I couldn't stop myself. 'Do you miss her?'

'All the time, that's why I got Darth. I need company.'

The dog must have heard his name mentioned because, with skidding paws on the floor and climbing claws on my dress, he was up against my body pinning me to the fridge. His teeth were bared, his ears raised, and low growls seeped from his throat.

'Down boy, she's a visitor,' said Zed.

I stood rigid, my back pressed on the fridge, wondering whether the dog could reach my face.

'He's only a puppy,' said Zed.

'He looks huge to me.'

Zed whistled, and Darth sank to the ground, sidling towards him, whining. The dog slung me a backward glance. His yellow eyes were loco.

'Do you like Leonard Cohen?' asked Zed.

'I do.'

Swinging a six-pack, Zed led the way back to the living room. Darth's claws clipped the wooden floor behind us. He growled at me every opportunity then lay quietly, chewing the corner of a rug.

'Maria's favourite song was Suzanne,' said Zed. He played the track three times, pouring beer in his stomach and tears from his eyes.

I knew how he felt – Maria was gone for eternity – so I wept too, for both of us.

We sobbed while he rolled a joint. When the weed kicked in, we danced. The music came alive, the Sisters of Mercy joined in, jiving, shining, and blessing us. Zed was sweating. He smelt sour like last night's beer.

Darth lolled on the floor next to me. He lay on his back with his rear legs pointing at the ceiling and his front legs hanging sideways. His mouth sagged open and his teeth clenched together in sharp points. He was either stoned or dead.

When the dope wore off, we ate a pack of Oreos and drank more Budweiser. I can't remember how it happened, but afterwards our clothes lay on the floor and we were bucking on the bed. The sun burnt my eyes so Zed drew the drapes, and zigzag patterns still shimmered on the rim of my vison. And Leonard Cohen's voice still pulled my insides out. Zed knelt over me. His arms, legs, chest, and belly were covered with marmalade fuzz. We swung around the room clinging to one another. I was having sex with an Orang-utang.

'I love you, Suzanne,' he said.

'I'm Jade.'

'Let's get married.'

'You've already got a wife.'

'Maria's gone.'

'She'll be back.'

'She can't.'

'Why not?'

'I may've hurt her.'

For some reason, I found this funny. I began to laugh. I squawked and snorted until I cried.

Zed's pale eyes were flat and empty. His face was speckled with freckles, his lips too. His skin was soft and smooth as glass. He looked about fifteen years old.

'How old are you?' I said, after whatever I was laughing at had passed.

'Twenty-one,' he said. 'What about you?'

'Thirty-five,' I said, feeling much older than that. I was as aged as the crumbling shed at the back of my yard. I suffered from all the ailments that snare old women, wrinkles, cellulite, scars, and heavy periods. I was held together by black netting like the strawberry plants crawling in front of the shed.

'Wow,' he said, 'you're almost as old as my mom.'

Something dark came down between us like a shutter. A taboo, so bitter I could taste it. I lit a cigarette and watched the smoke drift around my face.

'Tell me about Maria?'

'She finished high school but couldn't afford college. I guess she was too smart for me. She wanted to go sideways.'

My husband and I also went sideways. I wanted babies and he wanted other women.

'How did she pass her time?'

'She typed letters for lawyers all day. By the time she got home at night, I needed her real bad. But all she cared for was reading books.'

The flesh under his eye was pulsing again.

'The trouble with her was she thought too much.'

Zed opened a beer can. 'I knew she was full of shit,' he said, 'so, I drank. I drank till I lost it.'

I also lost it, the day I came home and found my husband in our bed with my friend. On that same day I lost everything, my youth, my marriage, and my future life.

The room rocked, tipping me off the bed. I crawled to the bathroom with Darth behind, yelping and nipping at my ankles. I leaned over the bowl, and every time I vomited the dog tried to push me into the toilet. Then I limped back to bed, empty as a tunnel.

Zed was asleep and I lay next to him. Bumps sprung up on my legs and back, itching like crazy. I must have caught the dog's fleas. I scratched till my skin tore.

Darth settled on the floor next to the bed and was quiet except for occasional chewing noises.

I must have passed out.

It was dark as treacle when I woke. I prodded Zed. He sat up, grabbed my arms and shook me, cursing Maria, saying he was going to kill her. His spit flew in my face. Darth barked furiously, body soaring, paws scraping the side of the bed. Zed looked dazed till his mind returned.

'It's you,' he said. 'What do you want?'

'I want to go home,' I said.

'Sure,' said Zed, covering his eyes with his hands as if there was something he didn't want to look at.

He unfolded his naked body and stood sideways next to the bed. I watched him pull on his briefs and zip up his jeans. He bent to pick up my dress. It hung from his hands in shreds.

'I'm sorry,' he said, thrashing Darth who slunk under the chair whimpering. Zed gave me a tracksuit to wear for the ride back. I rolled up the legs and sleeves.

'I'll buy you another one of these dresses,' he said. 'Where'd you get it?'

'It didn't fit me,' I said.

Joy

Katie Martin

www.twitter.com/K_A_Martin

Wednesday's the best night of the week because I spend it with my friend Sherry. 6-8 o'clock is Pa's REACH session and also Women's Bible Study, which means Collin and Keith Jnr are at boys' worship with Pa, and Mom's busy reading the Book with Mrs Koonar. They're on Ecclesiastes right now and Mom's trying to get Mrs Koonar to understand that when Solomon drinks too hard, that's bad, but when he works too hard that's bad too. And that when he fornicates for fornication's sake, that's real bad. Upshot is, Solomon "misses the mark" until Chapter 11 but Mrs Koonar don't get it. She'd not say so, but Mom despairs of Mrs Koonar. She keeps pets, and not dogs neither, but two black cats the size of bob-deer. She treats them no different than children and she doesn't eat meat. Mrs Koonar reckons people are animals too, but the Lord says different, which is why we're made in His image and why eating meat's our Holy duty.

Anyways, Wednesday's Sherry's mom works late at the diner in town, Mom's busy saving Mrs Koonar and I'm in charge of Julie and Lizbeth. My twin sisters are no trouble. I just tuck them into their cribs, turn on Dr David Jeremiah nice and low, and once they're asleep Sherry and I sit out on my back porch and talk some over a packet of Buc-ee's beaver nuggets.

It's June and not quite dark yet. There's a scuffling at the back of the yard, a coyote hunting for scraps most likely. Pa's REACH group are singing: Jehovah reigns, he dwells in light.

'Nature and time quite naked lie,' I hum.

Sherry bites down on a Buc-ee's. A couple of corn-crumbs hit my leg and one of them lands on my knee. I flick it off. 'Like Mr Coker and Miss Stoner,' she says. 'They quite naked lie.'

She's got to know I won't be able to resist that. 'Mr Coker's your math professor, right?'

Sherry nods. 'Uh-huh. And married to Mrs Coker and with three kids and another on the way.'

'Fornication for fornication's sake,' I say, because that's what I guess Mom might have said. And Sherry curls over, laughing hard, and I feel kind of bad that I've mocked Mom, even by accident. I reach for a Buc-ee's but Sherry's pulled the pack away.

I wonder what Mr Coker looks like. And Miss Stoner. And poor old Mrs Coker. I reckon I can visualize her, all big with baby and struggling with a double-stroller as the veins pop purple out of her ankles. Mom got that way with Julie and Lizbeth.

'In fact,' Sherry says, 'it's what Irven Devore calls "sex"'.

'Irven Dewho?'

'Irven Devore.' She says it like it's exotic. It is exotic. 'Irven Devore is an anthropologist.' She says the word carefully, turning it into about a hundred syllables, and I try to look like I know what an anthropologist is. 'They study all kinds of animals, including people.'

I don't correct her because I'm not Mom. Besides, I'm still feeling kind of sorry for Mrs Coker.

'He's written books about it. And,' she continues, offering up some more Buc-ee's now the packet's nearly empty, 'he demonstrates sex in class. Actually does it. Sex. Right there, like in front of the total class. He's awesome.'

Sherry sighs and stretches out her long brown legs. I covet them. Mine are short and stumpy as a pair of post-oaks.

'Lions have sex 3500 times for every baby lion they make.' She says it matter of fact, like she's the lady on TV who gives out tornado warnings. Then she tips the packet up to her mouth. I hear the crumbs hit her tongue and bubble there like popping candy. She screws up the bag, tosses it into the yard. The coyote scuffle over by the mesquite. 'That's what Irven Devore says.'

I don't care about Mr Coker and Miss Stoner anymore. I nearly don't care about Mrs Coker and her fat ankles. I want to know about Irven Devore. I want to be at school in Henrietta with Sherry, watching him do sex.

I want to, and I don't want to.

'So how does he do it? The sex?'

Sherry shrugs like it's a lame question. Maybe it is. 'Oh,' she says. 'You know.'

Oftentimes Wednesdays are the best days, but I don't know, which is why I asked and now Sherry seems cranky. It's not even 7 o'clock when she stands, stretches those crazy-long legs and brushes down her shorts. 'Better be getting back.'

My name is Allyson Joy Priddy. Allyson after Mom's mom, Joy because of the joy my family finds in our Lord and Savior, but also because that's where we live. Joy, Texas, population 100 (including us).You might've heard of Clay County, but I'm guessing you'll not have heard of Joy. Why would you've?

First-off, introductions. Deborah – that's my mom. My pa's called Keith, but we call him Pa. To the 93 other folks who live in Joy, he's Pastor Priddy. Then there's my little brothers Collin and Keith Jnr and twin baby sisters Julie and Lizbeth. And then there's me, Allyson Joy, 11 years and 10 months of age.

Six months of the year Joy is hot. And I'm talking crazy-mean smack-in-the face hot. Hot that'd melt asphalt if the roads here had any, hot that makes coyote howl and loop-the-loop after their own tails 'til the heat wins out and pulls them down into furzy heaps on the earth. In our house ceiling fans whorl and though Pa's rigged up a generator Mom calls "near-on air-con" I'd swear it just bangs and cranks. It's still as heavy inside as out.

Pa met Mom at Church in Wichita Falls: 'I knew straight-off he was the one for me, the Good Lord meant it to be.' Mom often talks in rhyme, which might be because she reads The Berenstein Bears Say Their Prayers aloud every day. I'm home-schooled, and Julie and Lizbeth will be too. Only the boys get real school. And Sherry, of course, but Sherry's different - her mom hasn't welcomed the Lord into her life.

Joy is the sort of place you don't get out of. Aside from the school bus that comes on a weekday and picks up Collin, Keith Jnr and Sherry, you can go whole days without seeing one single vehicle. My bedroom's the attic - hottest room in the house. Open the door and it's like the heat must've rounded up its very own congregation and they're all in my room, begging for the mercy of the Lord, rising up in one giant Hallelujah from floor to sloping roof and filling that space so tight oftentimes I worry if Mom and Pa's ceiling can take the weight. And looking out of my window you'd think the prairie must roll on to the edge of the very world.

One day I want to see the ocean.

Sherry was 12 last Fall, but when you're short on company an age gap don't matter so much. Mom and Pa don't rate Sherry's mom, but they let me visit on her birthday. We had apple and cinnamon pie and Sherry's mom drank beer out of the bottle and laughed a lot. Sherry's pa's with the Lord and she's got no brothers or sisters, so you might think she'd get lonesome, but she reads. She reads a lot.

Sherry's not seen the ocean neither, but she says she will – 'Maybe once I'm at Harvard'.

Somehow when Sherry says things, you just believe them. In Henrietta she learns biology, chemistry and math, proper math. Math where you've got formulas and when you use them, the answers come out right every time. Mom teaches home-baking math and seamstress math, which is what her mom taught her.

Thursday afternoon's Mom drives us girls to the Edwards public library in Henrietta. She bundles the twins into the back and I sit up front with her. A fug of dust rises up from the wheels, and if you didn't know town was just 16 miles away behind that row of trees you'd be forgiven for thinking Joy Shannon Road went on forever. I'm happiest when we're past the post-oaks, when I see other cars, huddles of buildings, the church spire. The smell of gasoline and the growl of a passing Hummer make my chest go tight.

Sherry'll be in class now. I picture her in a huge auditorium, chewing hard at her pencil as she watches Irven Devore. Thrusting. 'And this, class, is how it's done. Do we have a volunteer amongst you?' Sherry's got moxie as well as brains, so she'll be raising her arm, spittle-soaked pencil extending excited fingers. 'Me, sir!'...

'Amen!' Mom grinds the car to a stop.

The library has a dedicated Christian section but Mom lets me borrow "classics" too. She thinks I'll get bored and decide I prefer the Book (and for a while, I did just that - blame Moby Dick). But today Mom's distracted. Julie's starting a fever and Lizbeth's stiffening into one of her tantrums, wants out of her stroller.

I murmur thanks to the Lord, skidaddle from Christian, dodge past Classics and into Anthropology.

'He's not at your school,' I tell Sherry next Wednesday. She's not brought snacks, so I worry she's still antsy.

'Who?'

'Irven Devore.'

'I know.'

'So why does he matter?'

She rolls her eyes and looks up from picking at her cuticle. 'Because he's at Harvard and he's from here.'

From here? 'I got a book of his,' I say.

'You did? Which one? Show!'

Pleased she's pleased, I jump off of the porch and she follows me up to my room. I open the door and she makes a noise like a balloon going down. The heat'll do that.

When I pull out the book Sherry sheeshes and shakes her head. 'You keep Irven under your pillow. That's wild.' She snatches it from me and flips to the back fly-leaf. 'So you read this bit, right?' Wrong. We huddle beside the window. Hot indigo light pours over us. She points at the text and her nails have tiny gold stars glued on. I covet her nails too, but coveting is "missing the mark".

"Irven Devore, born in Joy, Texas, ("population 8", as he calls it) is the oldest son of a Methodist minister. Now a devout atheist, he's "swapped the Bible for Darwin". Applications for his Harvard class, Science B-29 (popularly known as "sex class") are consistently over-subscribed."

Joy's not the sort of place you get out of. Unless you're Irven Devore.

Or Sherry.

Sherry saw the ocean. She sent me postcards of it.

But her last postcard wasn't of the ocean. It was of a red-brick building and, beneath it, Harvard's coat of arms.

Sherry wrote me that her course was going well. She'd had a boyfriend, Karl from New England, who she'd broken up with (he was a distraction, apparently). She'd aced her freshman year and was on the wait list for Class B-29.

I wrote her back. A long letter, full of questions. I mentioned Pa's death only in passing and omitted Mom's illness. I'd started to write her about our new pastor, Pastor Darwin, knowing she'd enjoy the joke, but I had to sign off in a hurry and struck-out the joke as disrespectful. I was late for Women's Bible Study. It was Wednesday.

Maybe there were too many questions in that letter and the thought of answering them tired her. Maybe answering would have been a distraction, like Karl from New England. Or maybe my letter never made it – it's a long journey from Joy, Texas to Cambridge, Massachusetts, and so many places one might get lost along the way.

The Woman on Wednesday's

Emma Norry

www.linkedin.com/pub/emma-norry/81/851/230

As the lights gradually come up, people squint and gather their bags. When the majority have gone, you step out into the carpeted aisle and that's when you recognise her, slightly ahead of you. She was here last week. And two weeks before that, too. Here being Senior Screen, which you come to every Wednesday at eleven at The Odeon. She's about sixty, twenty years older than you and at least twenty years younger than the average Senior Screen member.

The way she carries herself with a casual yet practised elegance intrigues you, reminds you of someone though you can't think exactly who.

You've seen regulars before, in the foyer before the film starts, dunking their biscuits into free cups of tea. You never indulge in the biscuits, only sip hot black coffee and discreetly click in the sweeteners you carry in your handbag. No-one speaks to you, although this week (your seventh), you receive a few nods and the occasional smile. You wonder what, if anything, they think about a woman at least forty years their junior with nothing better to do on a weekday.

You'd gladly tell them if they asked. You'd love to share your enthusiasm for Katherine Hepburn, Humphrey Bogart, Spencer Tracey, Rita Heyworth; those stars of the 1940's who transport you in a way modern stars never do. After the lights come up, you always linger, hoping this week the hand of friendship might be extended; but it never is.

She holds the door open, here's your chance.

"Wh- what did you think?" Your voice cracks through lack of use.

You haven't spoken since six p.m. yesterday when you reminded a colleague you'd be off today. You share a tiny office with two men close to retirement. You don't say much.

Dave didn't even look up from his monitor.

"How's that satisfying, using up all your leave like that, one day at a time?"

You don't need a conventional break because you've no family. You've chosen twenty-five weeks working a four day week.

"What did I think?" Her voice is soft and cultured. Physically, she brings to mind a weeping willow. Her makeup is subtle - fine, dusky pinks. Ash blonde hair in a neat bob just above her shoulders. A cream silk blouse complements navy trousers and cream, low-heels. You're conscious of your tracksuit bottoms.

When her voice hits your ear-drum, you feel a blast of deja vu.

She sighs. "Wasn't it charming?"

What to say next? Volunteer an opinion or ask about what she's just said? Too many variables – brain shuts down. Verbally, she reaches out before you stumble.

"How simple everything seems back then. Lovely."

Her eyes are - she's been crying. You want to touch her arm, offer something of comfort.

"Have you been to these screenings before?" she asks.

And suddenly, it's like she's turned around a road works sign and it says Go, and you can't stop your mouth from flapping and the rusty engine of your voice springs into life.

"I come every week. The old ones are the best. It's a nice break from the little ones, they're four and two. They're in nursery. After the film, I treat myself to lunch, you know, a bit of 'me time' before going home and getting dinner ready for my – my – husband."

You've no idea why the torrent from your lips is all lies.

Moving down the corridor, the foyer entrance approaches and daylight hurtles towards both of you. The black and white images and sassy humour retreat, you long to drag them back kicking and screaming because you want to talk further but there's no reason to, there's no point of reference, now. But then she says, "Are you coming next week?"

You nod.

Staring at you, head tilted to one side, she says kindly, "Until then... then!"

It's a statement, not a question and before you can reply she's gone, heels clicking on the polished marble tiles.

Apart from Wednesdays, you adhere to a strict routine. You rise at six a.m. and run for forty minutes. At your desk by nine a.m., leave the office at six p.m., home by seven p.m. You eat whilst listening to the radio until ten-thirty p.m. After washing up, you're in bed by eleven p.m. It's been the same for ten years, although the Wednesdays are a new addition. After insisting to the doctor that anti-depressants weren't the answer, he rhapsodised about beaches, palm trees, sunshine, but you couldn't imagine anything worse.

Seeing the advert for classic films, you thought you'd give it a try and it became another habit before you knew it.

The next Wednesday you're early. You sip the free coffee – too hot, too weak – and smile gingerly at the regulars. She's not amongst the throng.

As the opening credits roll, you see her fumble for her seat in the dim light. You sit back, though you've now lost all interest in the film. You've dressed formally today, and the waistband of your trousers digs in. She's all you can think about. You don't know her name but you've been practising asking. Even at primary school, it was never easy for you. Saying 'Hi' was too hard – those variables, again.

When the lights come up, she seeks you out.

"Hello again." Today she's in lilac; a shift dress and matching cardigan. Her eyes are bright blue; they remind you of a blue topaz ring your mother left you.

"I realised last week I didn't introduce myself. I'm Deborah." Her hand is extended. Pale skin, faint age spots, light raised veins; short manicured nails. Before thoughts invade and paralyse, you act quickly, but you're a fraction too late or perhaps it's too early - you've misjudged shaking her hand and so she pulls hers up, away, back and when your fingertips touch; there's a spark; a tiny 'ping' of electricity.

Her laugh is light and mischievous. "Shall we go for coffee?"

Something about her emboldens you. Coffee at the café next door it is.

You've never known someone to ask so many questions.

"Where are you from? How long have you been married? Are your family nearby? Do you work? What are your children called?"

If only you could change what you'd first said. Because now you have to spew more lies and suddenly you have a whole history and not one you'd ever given any thought to, either. As you describe your fictions: your husband, Dan (married for thirteen years) and lovely children, Marta and Jamie. Mum, dad and three sisters all live on the Isle of Wight, you're aware of what could have been, what you might be missing.

When it's her turn to speak, you're relieved and sit back. Her voice is like listening to chamber music. She and her husband Jim moved here a year ago. She misses Islington, but London's a young person's city, isn't it? You nod, even though you've never been.

They have four sons, but they all live abroad. Paul's married and his wife's expecting. She feels too young to be grandma – nanny, she thinks – but of course she's delighted. She might go over to New Zealand after the baby arrives. Then there's Simon, who's a painter, Thomas the musician and William, who's volunteering in Uganda. Shame you're taken! She laughs.

"Oh! I hope I haven't offended you! Sorry, just a little joke." She chews her lower lip and offers a small smile. Her eyes dart to the clock above the counter.

You focus hard on a stain on the varnished table. Then she says, "I always felt outnumbered in our house – all those boys, and I've two brothers myself. So, what's it like coming from a family of girls? Tell me about your sisters."

So, you invent. But this time, unlike Dan or the children, this one's easy. This feels real, could be real because it's something you've dreamt about. So you tell her all about Katie and Anne and Jo (named after children's classics, as your parents were such voracious readers), how there are roughly three years between you. You're the youngest and the only one with children.

Deborah nods and never takes her eyes off you all the while you're talking. You can't see anyone else but her. But then she checks the clock and reaches for her handbag.

"Oh. I'm so sorry but I have to go. I have an appointment. It's been lovely talking with you." She pushes her chair back.

"It's Bogart and Bacall next week!" she says, and she's gone.

It's one-thirty p.m. and the empty tables fill up with people on lunch breaks.

A heavy set man in dirty overalls grabs Deborah's chair, "You using this?" He doesn't wait for the reply. You're on your own. Alone. And everyone can see. Panic shakes you by the throat.

The week after, Deborah's not at Senior Screen. You've no recollection of the film that showed.

The last time you see her, she's by the table, watching the pensioners gobble up their bourbon biscuits. She's in cornflower blue. Seeing you in the ticket queue, she waves and her smile is so warm you feel the heat across the room.

After the film where you sit together, she suggests lunch.

"I'm sorry I had to rush off last time we met. Jim suffers from Alzheimer's. He's in a care home down the road." She pushes her goat cheese salad around her plate. "I usually visit him before the screening, and then sometimes again after."

The pause is too long whilst your brain scrambles through all the responses that may be appropriate to her disclosure. Your mouth doesn't alight on any of them.

She takes a sip of her orange juice. "Did you enjoy the film today?"

"Oh, yes. Fred Astaire could really move, couldn't he?"

"Don't forget – Ginger did everything he did. Backwards, and in heels!"

Her laugh should be bottled.

You can't stop thinking about her, everything she says. She's like the perfect family member. Your parents were decent. You weren't beaten or abused. Your mum was just… absent. Physically she was there, but the dark moods dad used to call the 'blackies' would mean she'd disappear off, or retreat to her bed for days, sometimes weeks. Aged thirteen you swapped Jane Eyre for Jane Asher. Instead of drinking or dancing or drugs, you washed and ironed dad's uniform, went food shopping, made sure the bills were paid. Someone had to, your dad worked twelve hour days to ensure that the house wasn't repossessed.

You and dad never spoke much either. He probably didn't know what to say. He was an old dad compared to everyone else's. Fifty by the time you arrived. He was a quiet man, composed of shadows and empty space.

You never see Deborah again. One lunch. Two coffees. A privileged glimpse into the intricacies of friendship. Maybe Deborah will return to

Senior Screen again but you don't, because your months of free Wednesdays come to an end.

You bake yourself a fantastic cake for your fortieth and get a companion; a tortoiseshell kitten from a cat shelter. You name him Titus.

It's the only care home within twenty miles of the cinema. You lingered in the car park, couldn't see her Nissan.

When you press the entry buzzer, you don't know if you've planned this. Would it – does it – matter?

"Here to see Jim? Oh. How lovely, you must be..." the care assistant – so young that surely the possibility of death, disease, decay has never occurred to her – doesn't put you through the rigorous security you imagined might exist.

"His daughter-in-law."

The door handle feels weighty as you pull it open, balancing the sunflowers in the crook of your other arm.

You're just bursting with things to say to him.

The Ideal Cottage

Alex Reece Abbott

www.alexreeceabbott.info

It's love at first sight. Worn stone walls splattered with soft grey lichens, neat overlapping slate tiles puffy with moss. Indicators of superior air quality, thinks Molly.

The cottage rests on a narrow grassy point at edge of the village. No neighbours.

Held in a firm embrace by thick dry-stone walls, there's a wooden gate that leads – and she particularly likes this – out onto the narrow snaking path that edges the rocky coastline to the headland. The cottage sings to her of privacy and the quiet life she's yearning for.

The agent obligingly fast-tracks the purchase so she completes before the end of her holiday, outbidding stiff competition and beating some local who's always hankered after the place.

After she moves in, occasional disembodied walkers bob past, only their heads visible above her dry-stone girdle. She comes to recognise her regulars. Sometimes she hears barking.

It's a week or so before she notices the dog shit. Not from Bonnie, her perfectly trained Jack Russell. Not an occasional stray deposit. Her cottage is encircled by dark coils of dog dirt, moist little mounds and odd drying lozenges. Her anger surges, fierce as the spring equinox.

How come she never noticed all these cairns of crap before? Surely they're an aberration; incomers – a weekend walking group from the city. The next morning, she marches with Bonnie to the headland. The old globs of dog dirt are still festering but there, against the base of her stone wall, new deposits are soiling the grass verge.

She photographs the shit on her phone.

She walks, surrounded by spring beauty – the rugged cliffs, the millpond blue firth, primroses flowering soft yellow, pure snowdrops dotting the hills white. Dolphins porpoise and spy-hop – but mostly she sees the dollops of brown dog-shit deposited along the path.

The little point where her cottage perches is clearly in the ascendance as the preferred village dog-toilet. Determined not to let the ignorance of a few irresponsible dog owners spoil her ideal home, she watches out for possible perpetrators but the dry-stone wall blocks her view – she glimpses walkers, she can't see their dogs.

She keeps a journal, photographing the latest deposits and logging them every day.

The territorial squabble escalates; the more the dogs do, the more other dogs are compelled to overlay their scents. After a week, she decides that she's surrounded by persistent offenders. She calls the estate agent. He pleads ignorance on canine faecal fouling and wishes her well.

Molly writes a message on her laptop, heading it POLITE NOTICE. She adds a clip-art spotted hound of Snoopy-esque cuteness for the right balance of firm request and humour. She laminates the sign and pins it to her gate so walkers can see it as they start the path.

She waits. The mounds mount and fester around her cottage. There is no obvious decrease in canine bowel activity in her vicinity. No-one knocks on her door to request a free poo-bag. No-one volunteers their name or address, so she cannot fulfil the second part of her reciprocal offer: for Bonnie to go and void her bowels at the fouler's own gate.

Bonnie has grown complacent, rarely even barking back at passing dogs. Molly wonders if she's depressed. If a dog's sense of smell truly is ten million times more sensitive than a human's, then she must be in Dog Hell.

She writes to the Council. Due to budget cuts, the dog warden sends a single lurid poster which threatens foulers with a forty pound fine, even if they offend in the dark.

She laminates the poster and puts it on the telegraph pole at the head of the path.

The next week, the dog warden sends her a No Fouling sign which contradicts the poster, and threatens a maximum five hundred pound fine for anyone who doesn't bag and bin their dog waste. She nails it to the telegraph pole too.

At the weekend, Molly buys an aerosol of paint from the general store, a shouty shade of fluorescent orange. Morning and night, she patrols. After she paints the piles of poo, they look like alien abstract art installations on the verge. No-one comments.

Her tally of the deposits demonstrates that this week's accumulated bowel evacuations could have earned the Council nine thousand pounds in fines. She advises the dog warden. He comes and installs a brand-new bright red dog-poo bin about ten feet from her cottage wall. Then he stands around admiring her view and chatting, taking long angry drags from his cigarette like he's sucking venom from a wound.

She sleeps badly, regularly peering out her bedroom window, unable to see much unless it's a full moon. With her mail-order night-vision glasses, she spots a mole, a vole, three rabbits and two gulls. No walkers. No dogs.

According to her next record-breaking count, the Council could have earned around thirteen thousand and five hundred pounds that week. She pens another plea to walkers, then laminates it and pins it on the pole, under the official penalty notices.

Her last sign says For Sale. She knows that the villagers all blether about her private war but she removes all the dog-poo notices anyway, in case they deter any buyers. She wants out and the cottage sells immediately for a knock-down price. She moves to a bungalow off the beaten track and up a long drive. It isn't ideal. The views of the firth aren't as good but the air's okay and there's a lot less shit to deal with.

After she settles in, she pines for the headland. One morning she walks Bonnie along the path. No-one's bothered to replace her signs and the ugly red plastic bin has gone now too, yet the path is remarkably unfouled. On her old wooden gate, there's a new sign: Chien lunatique.

There's a man in her front garden, leaning over her dry-stone wall, blowing smoke rings as he gazes out to the tranquil firth.

"Hello," says the dog warden.

Red

Julie Lockwood

We called her Red. I didn't realise for years that it was because her real name was Ruth. I saw the town's name on the back of a lorry recently and finally got it, after all those years – it was a joke, a West Country attempt at humour - Redruth. She had never been Red in the papers though, or on the television. She was always "Missing Devon Schoolgirl Ruth Parton" there.

She would have been fifty one now. Or is fifty one. I haven't known for a long time what tense to put her in. I haven't seen her since she was eleven, no one has. Well, not that we know of. But I have thought about her. Every day. She disappeared, vanished into the ether as she walked up the road from the village, passed our house and on up the lane. I saw her, spoke to her, and then she was gone.

There were theories. Still are, UFOs, paedophiles, her dad, but nothing ever comes of them. Her face was on the front pages again recently, it was the fortieth anniversary of the day she went. She looked like we all looked then, badly cut hair and skinny as a wraith. And like an eleven year old should - knee high socks, pleated skirt, buttoned up cardigan. The distillation of timeless innocence. Only she wasn't. You can still see, around the edges of her eyes, that determined look, that probing stare that sought out weak spots that she could poke and probe and whittle away at until you were just a vacuum. Next to the photos of her, as there always was back then, was a picture of her watch. The distinctive turquoise Timex that she proudly wore - and shoved under our faces, pointing out how much better it was than anything we might, or would ever, own. The watch that the police hoped might be the clue to her disappearance.

The watch I have just found. Four decades on and it is still unmistakable. And here it is, curled like a kitten in a box under my father's bed. At first

I just stare at it, my heart, a thumping slab of meat, beats loudly in my ears. Beneath it, my stomach rises and lurches like a frightened shoal of mackerel. I want to faint but I know that what I am looking at is too important for that. I reach out a hand towards it, but I am too scared to touch it. It looks the same as it always did, but smaller, more vulnerable, sad. I try to ignore it, for now at least, and look at the other things in the box as if I am picking primroses from around a coiled, sleeping adder. There is a photo of my mother, younger than I am now, topless, kneeling on a brown patterned bedspread wearing a self-conscious smile and pushing her unsubstantial breasts together with her shoulders; a rusted locket with a scrap of wiry hair curled inside; a couple of baby teeth. I pick up a tooth instead of the watch. It is easier. I assume it is mine but then a thought comes pushing into my brain that it might not be mine, it might be Red's. And I drop it back in as if it is alive.

Then I think I shouldn't touch the watch because it might be evidence. But I cannot think why my father would have it. I think it must be a mistake, he must have found it somewhere, maybe he thought it was mine? Or perhaps he found it, out on the common, in those early days when great lines of villagers walked slowly across the open spaces, poking into the undergrowth with sticks looking for clues or a body or both and us kids ran around in packs like excited terriers, the part fear part excitement feeling driving us into a frenzy. He must have just forgotten to hand it in. I think I need to do it for him.

Very carefully, holding just the very points of the corners I take the photo of my mother out and place it upside down on my father's bedside cabinet next to his pill dispenser and the pot where his dentures should be. Then I take the box, put the lid on and very slowly walk to my car.

At the police station a uniformed youth with an acne blasted face looks vacantly at me.

"I have something that is Red's," I mutter.

"You've got something red?" he asks, dismissively.

"I mean, Ruth's," I say. "Something that is Ruth's."

"Well, can you give it back to her?"

I begin to tell him why I can't but then a drunk man with an open gash on his forehead comes into the tiny waiting room and heaves a perfect Venn diagram of vomit onto the floor.

The policeman swears, loudly and openly, and there is a lot of fussing around as he attempts to deal with the man and clean the floor so I move to a hard plastic seat, put the box on my lap and wait.

I think about how Red disappearance changed our childhoods. We weren't turfed out of the house for the day anymore, expected to roam for hours on our bikes and drink water out of springs. Instead we were allowed to stay at home and watch the Banana Splits and old Tarzan films on the television. It was great.

It made people suspicious though and I think that has always stayed with me, the constant need to explain myself. I had been one of the last to see her. In the morning I was in the front garden and I saw her go past on her way in to the village. She didn't see me, or pretended she didn't and I was pleased because I was scared of her, everyone was. Even the boys. I had chicken pox so I wasn't allowed out into the lane. Later on I was sitting on our gate waiting for something to happen and she came past again. She jabbed a spikey nail into one of my blistering spots. It hurt but I didn't say so. Then she scooped out some of the watery liquid and licked it off the top of her finger. She told me I was even uglier than normal and everyone would hate me even more. She said you could die of chicken pox and that she hoped I would.

Then my mum shouted down to me that dinner was ready. I was pleased because I could go and because it was Saturday so it was sausage and chips.

"Tell her to fuck off," demanded Red. "Go on, say it! Shout it!"

I stood looking at her, slack mouthed.

"Say it, you baby. Say 'Fuck off you bitch!' Go on. If you don't, I'll torture you." She grabbed my arm and twisted it hard with both her hands, I could feel the burn in my bone. It hurt and I thought for one terrible moment I would wet myself. There was a scribble of a noise and my dad appeared from around the corner. She dropped my arm immediately and pretended to smile at me. His eyes skirted over me and he looked deeply at her.

"Hello!" said Red, all nice and polite.

"Inside!" he barked at me. I saw the smug look of triumph on her face as I turned and ran.

I ate my dinner quickly because I was scared I would be in trouble with dad. I wasn't sure why I would be but there often was no reason for trouble. He didn't come in though and mum put his plate in the grill to keep warm.

I said I was tired and went and lay on my bed and read some old Beanos and Upper Fourth at Malory Towers and scratched my spots. I think I fell asleep for a bit. When I woke up the light in the bedroom was a soupy colour and I could hear the deep rumble of unfamiliar voices.

I went downstairs, bleary eyed. There was a policeman there. He asked me about seeing Red and I told him it was just before dinner. He didn't talk for long because I started coughing and so my dad took me to the kitchen to get a drink.

"If he asks you what time we have dinner, say six o'clock," he whispered. "Posh people have dinner in the evening. If he thinks we aren't posh then we might be in trouble. Posh people don't get into trouble."

I nodded and sipped my squash. Then he told me I wasn't allowed to say anything mean about Red because something bad might have happened to her and you couldn't be nasty about people who bad things had happened to because that wasn't fair. I had to say she was my friend. I told the same story to several different policeman over the following days and in the end it all got a bit jumbled in my brain and made my head ache and my spots itch.

Gradually, the village absorbed Red's disappearance. On the surface, it opened out and let in all the police and the press and people appeared on the television talking about her and what a terrible thing it was and how distraught we all were. But underneath it got on with things - children weren't allowed to wander around on their own much but other than that the same things happened. People died and got married and had babies and the Flower Show still happened on the first weekend in August and the men still got loud and leery in the pub and the women still ran jumble sales and gossiped outside the village shop. Red's mum, who was always a bit odd didn't leave the house unless she had to and she no one was surprised when she died a few years later.   Three months after that her father married the barmaid from the Red Lion.

I left home as soon as I could. My family had never been quite functional, although we didn't know that word back then. Dad had always knocked mum, and sometimes me, around a bit. He drank too much, expected too much. I visited them occasionally over the years but his dark moods still bruised the atmosphere. After mum died and he had fallen ill we did become closer, he became softer around the edges, easier to deal with and I started to visit regularly. Last week I arrived not long after he had fallen in the bathroom and broken his hip. I called the ambulance and held his hand all the way to the hospital. I was there when his heart stopped and when they called the crash team. I watched when they decided to stop shocking him with their paddles because he really was dead. Afterwards, I sat with him for a long time and told him that even though I had never said it when he was alive, I did love him.

As I sit in the police station reception with Red's watch in the box in front of me the obvious, glaring fact slaps me across the face. He loved me too. I hadn't known until that moment. But he had. He had loved me so much that he had killed Red for me.

I start to laugh, pick my way past the drunk man and the vomit and the muttering policeman. On the way home I unwind the car window, reach inside the box, pick out the watch and hurl it into the path of an oncoming lorry.

"Fuck off you bitch," I mutter through my tears.

How to Nudge Them Out of the Nest

Jacqueline Cooper

www.catelyncash.co.uk/

'It's not that I don't love my kids,' Carrie Miller complained to her friend in their lunch hour at work. 'I do. But now they've grown up, I'd love them a lot more if they would just move out and get a place of their own. Trust me, their 'best before' date has come and gone.' Glumly she stirred her coffee. 'The three of them treat the place like a hotel. I can't tell them off as they're supposedly adults, yet if I ask them to help around the house, they sulk like teenagers.'

Her friend Anna smiled enigmatically. 'Pushing them out the nest is easy,' she said.

Carrie shook her head. 'I can't just kick them out. Tom's had a major fall out with his girlfriend, David's putting money aside to go travelling and Ally's saving for a deposit for a house.' She sighed. 'I suppose I'll just have to stick it out a bit longer.'

Anna laughed. 'If do as I tell you, they'll be gone by the weekend. And even better, they'll think it was their idea. My plan worked a treat with my lot.'

Carrie thought of the tidy house she had left behind that morning, the untidy one she would no doubt be going home to tonight. Not to mention the pile of ironing everyone seemed to think was her job, and the meal for five she'd have to shop for and cook. She could see a life of drudgery stretching into her future. 'Okay. Tell me.'

So Anna did. And as she did Carrie's jaw dropped. 'No way! I could never do that!' she said, though the smile that spread across her face said otherwise.

Next morning, Carrie was running late. She popped two slices of toast in the toaster. No clean glass for her orange juice, even though she knew she had washed up before bed last night. Annoyed, she was rinsing a glass under the tap when her eldest son Tom strode in to the kitchen.

'Did you remember to pick up my dry cleaning, Mum?' he asked, helping himself to her toast which had just popped up.

'No, sorry, I had to take the dog to the vet.' Carrie put two more slices in the toaster. She poured herself a cup of tea then went to the fridge for the milk, shaking the carton which felt suspiciously light. 'Did you remember to buy milk?' Knowing the answer she tossed the empty carton in the bin, turning to catch him gulp down the juice she had just poured for herself.

Tom placed his dirty glass beside the sink. 'Forgot. Look, can you try and get it today? I'd go myself but I'm busy. Cheers, Mum. Bye.'

And I'm not busy? If he treated his girlfriend like that it was no wonder she'd kicked him out. 'Hang on! Can you take the dog out-' But she was talking to herself. The spaniel gazed at her with mournful eyes. 'Sorry, Chico, you'll have to wait.'

Her daughter Alison rushed into the kitchen like a whirlwind just in time to grab Carrie's toast from the toaster. 'Morning. What are we having for tea tonight?'

'What do you fancy?' asked Carrie, glumly watching her toast disappear for the second time.

'Anything,' Alison said. 'Except chicken. Or lamb chops. Or lasagne. Your lasagne's rubbish.'

Three staples crossed off plus an insult to her cooking. Carrie's mouth pursed but all she said was, 'I'll think of something. Can you take the dog out?'

'Seriously? In these shoes?' They both looked at her six inch red stilettos, which in Carrie's opinion were more suited to a brothel than the bank where Alison worked. 'See you later, Mum. I might bring some friends round so make something decent for tea, okay?'

Carrie made a face at the door swinging shut behind her.

Two more slices of toast in the toaster. Her husband John arrived just as they popped up. 'Toast. Great.' He looked around the kitchen. 'Where do we keep the orange juice?'

In the fridge? But it was easier just to get it so she did. 'Can you take the dog out before you go? I'm running late.'

'Of course, my sweet.' Cheerfully he opened the door and Chico shot into the garden.

'Not let! Take!' Carrie said but Chico was gone like a little black streak. 'Never mind,' she sighed, thinking I could have done that.

'See you later.' A kiss on the cheek and he too was gone.

Carrie dropped the last two slices of bread into the toaster just as David, her youngest, came in wearing his bike leathers. 'You still here, Mum? I thought you were going in early.' He put his crash helmet down on the table and opened the fridge to peer inside. 'Is this ham going free?' he asked, tearing the packet open with his teeth. The ham she had put aside for her lunch. He fished the half toasted bread out of the toaster and made himself a sandwich. 'Got to go. See you later Mum.' The door slammed.

'Wait!' Carrie called after him. 'The gate! Make sure it's shut-' Too late she saw Chico trotting down the road, head high. With a muttered curse she grabbed his lead and gave chase.

It took her half an hour to catch the dog. And exactly half that time for Carrie to decide to take Anna's advice.

By six o clock, Carrie was ready, nervous but determined. She had a steak pie in the oven and was peeling potatoes when she heard Tom's car. Too late to back out now. She braced herself with a fortifying gulp of wine.

'I forgot to get the milk again Mum, sorry- 'Tom stopped in his tracks and stared at Carrie.

She smiled breezily, though her heart was pounding. 'That's okay, love. I got it.'

Tom's eyes popped. 'Are you feeling alright, Mum?'

'Fine thanks, why?'

'Because...because...' he tailed off, speechless.

Carrie scooped the potatoes into the pot. 'Guess what? I've started a new health regime today. I'm an airatarian.'

'A what?' Tom looked at her as if she was speaking in tongues.

'An airatarian,' Carrie said, taking another sip of wine. 'Did you know the skin is the largest organ in the human body?' She looked down at the lime green bikini she was more bursting out of than squeezed into.

'Apparently the more skin you expose to the air, the more the body can detoxify. Look, I found those for your dad.' She indicated a pair of skimpy speedos on the back of a chair. 'They might be a bit tight but I'm sure he'll want to join me. Getting fit like this is so much easier than going to the gym, don't you think?'

Tom's horrified gaze flickered from her pale flesh to the straining bikini, to the tiny black speedos. 'How long are you going to be an airatarian?' he gulped.

'I'd like to lose a couple of stone at least,' Carrie said vaguely. 'In the summer I might discard the bikini altogether which should speed things up.'

The colour drained from Tom's face. 'I'm going upstairs.' He ducked out of the kitchen.

Well that had been excruciating. Carrie let out the breath she had been holding, though part of her felt he could have tried to look looked less horrified, considering her tummy had been tight as a drum before she'd had him.

She heard voices and laughter and only had seconds to brace herself with another slurp of wine before the door swung open again, on Ally this time. 'Mum that smells great. I brought some friends- Mother!'

Ally slammed the door and stood with her back to it, her friends on the other side. 'What on earth are you doing? Put some clothes on, right now!'

Carrie resented her tone. She wanted to say, consider this cellulite a timely warning of bad genes, my girl. What she did say was a cheery. 'Guess what? I'm an airatarian.'

'No.' Ally shook her head, not even waiting for an explanation. 'You're not. You are not walking about like that. My friends are here,' she hissed.

'There's plenty to go round,' said Carrie sweetly.

'You can say that again,' muttered Ally. She flounced out and Carrie heard her snap, 'Mum's having some kind of breakdown. We're going for a curry.'

Carrie took another generous slug of wine then checked the oven, wondering how airatarians managed to avoid kitchen burns. She'd just taken her oven gloves off when arms slid around her waist.

'I think I could get used to coming home to this.' John nuzzled her neck just as she heard David's motorbike.

'I'm disgusting the kids,' she explained hurriedly.

'I have no problem with that,' said John, still nuzzling. 'They've disgusted me often enough over the years.' He eyed her cleavage appreciatively. 'Can we disgust them some more by disappearing upstairs for a bit?'

She flapped him away with a tea towel. 'It's just David to go now. Go and get changed.' She handed him the speedos.

He held them up and raised an eyebrow. 'Okay. Then maybe you'll tell me what's going on?'

She was setting the table when David came in. 'That's a new look for you Mum,' he grinned.

'Get used to it.' She ate a potato and took a sip of wine. 'I'm an airatarian now. This is how I dress. Forever.'

David's eyes twinkled. 'Good for you. But I hate to tell you, airatarians don't eat. And they don't drink wine. They get all their energy from the sun.'

'They do?'

He kissed the top of her head. 'I won't tell. And don't worry, message understood loud and clear. I'll be moving in with my mates at the weekend.'

Result! Her phone beeped as he left. She reached for her pocket, but of course, she didn't have one, so hunted the phone down to read a message from Ally saying she wasn't coming home tonight, as she was going to look at a flat share with some friends.

Yes! The phone rang before she could put it down. This time it was Tom. 'Hi Mum. I'm going round to Sara's to see if we can patch things up. I won't be in for tea.'

'Good luck,' she said but he had already hung up.

'Carrie?' John called and she went to the bottom of the stairs. He was at the top wearing the tiny trunks and he struck a body builders pose. 'Want to come up and check the fit?'

She laughed. 'Just a minute,' she called and went back for the bottle of wine. The house to themselves, even just for an evening was a treat, but with a bit of luck, it looked like it could be for longer than that.

And all it took was a lime green bikini. And a lot of nerve.

About The Hysterectomy Association

The Hysterectomy Association provides impartial, timely and appropriate information and support to women. It was founded in the mid 1990's by Linda Parkinson-Hardman who is the author of several books about hysterectomy, online business and one novel.

It is based in Dorset in the UK and you can find out more about the association through the following accounts:

Website: hysterectomy-association.org.uk
Facebook: facebook.com/HysterectomyUK
Twitter: twitter.com/HysterectomyUK
LinkedIn: linkedin.com/company/the-hysterectomy-association

Other books from The Hysterectomy Association include:

- 101 Handy Hints for a Happy Hysterectomy
- In My Own Words: Women's Experience of Hysterectomy
- Losing the Woman Within
- The Pocket Guide to Hysterectomy
- A Diva's Guide to the Menopause - Short Story
- Hysteria 1
- Hysteria 2
- Hysteria 3

You can connect directly with Linda, our editor, on her blog at womanontheedgeofreality.com.